MW00412417

# *Love Letters of the Angels of Death*

# Love Letters of the Angels of Death

## JENNIFER QUIST

*a novel*

Copyright © 2013 Jennifer Quist
Second edition 2014.

All rights reserved. No part of this book may be reproduced,
for any reason or by any means without permission in writing
from the publisher.

Cover design: Debbie Geltner
Cover image: Warren Photographic
Book design: WildElement.ca
Author photo: Sara MacKenzie

LIBRARY AND ARCHIVES CANADA CATALOGUING IN PUBLICATION

Quist, Jennifer, author
Love letters of the angels of death : a novel / Jennifer Quist.
Issued in print and electronic formats.
ISBN: 9781927535158 (pbk.) ISBN: 9781927535165 (epub)
ISBN: 9781927535172 (mobi) ISBN: 9781927535189 (pdf)

I. Title

PS8633 U588 L69 2013     C813/.6 23  C2013-902009-8
                                     C2013-902010-1

Printed and bound in Canada by Imprimerie Gauvin.

Legal Deposit Library and Archives Canada
et Bibliothèque et Archives nationales du Québec.

Linda Leith Publishing acknowledges the support of the
Canada Council for the Arts.

Linda Leith Publishing Inc.
P.O. Box 322, Station Victoria,
Westmount, Quebec H3Z 2V8 Canada
leith.lindaleith@gmail.com
www.lindaleith.com

For Anders

# One

It was only a matter of time before we found human remains. Maybe that's true for everyone. This is how it happened for us.

The Earth is jammed with dead things. Everyone knows that. But this isn't just another day of tiptoeing through jelly fish on the beach or scrubbing smashed insects off the windshield. This is different. We aren't on a nature walk. We're in a small, dark enclosure made of spongy plywood and translucent, corrugated fibreglass. Mom calls it "the veranda" because she's actually kind of funny sometimes. The veranda is hammered together around the front step of her trailer. The trailer itself is right inside the gates of the Mountain View Mobile Home Community.

If it wasn't just a rental, and if I was a better son, I might have done something to try to make this place a little less grim. But I haven't.

Right now, it's the middle of the afternoon, it's windy hot, and the wooden slab behind the screen door of Mom's trailer is bolted shut. I've got one eye closed and I'm pressing my open eye up to the crack between the door and its frame. I can't see any-thing – not even the thinnest line of light from inside the trailer.

You are standing behind me, turned away from me to watch the driveway, still waiting for the man who rents Mom the trailer to meet us here with his morning star of dingy brass keys.

And it's early, early in another one of our pregnancies – the one we hope will be the final pregnancy of our marriage. You're at that stage where your sense of smell is more like a super power, so I step out of the way, nudging you toward the locked door, asking you to take an olfactory reading for us. But even after you sniff against the scruffy wood hard enough to make yourself cough, all you can say is, "Tobacco. Someone used to smoke out here – a lot – and I can't get past the tobacco."

It looks like we'll have some more time before the landlord gets here, so we stand in the veranda and go down the list again – Mom's parents, ex-husbands, my sisters and brother, the hospitals, police stations, her one friend who will still talk to her after the latest pyramid sales fiasco. We name all the people who've told us they haven't seen her for days.

"The window," you say.

I stand on the stringy, strip of quack grass – which Mom, in all earnestness, calls "the lawn" – and I watch you climb over the creosote-soaked salvaged railroad timbers and into the flowerbed outside the living room window. Mom isn't much of a gardener, so the bed is full of nothing but foxtails and variegated goutweed.

I hear you pronouncing a lame, weak curse on the vertical blinds hanging like a heavy, dirty, pleated skirt across the inside of the window. "Dang it. I can't see a dang thing."

From the lawn, I see Mom's neighbour standing up behind the window of the trailer next door to scowl out at you and your noise. If his dusty picture window weren't sealed, he'd be able to poke a broomstick out and touch the aluminum-clad wall of Mom's trailer. Maybe you see him too – scowl and everything. Maybe that's why you curl up your hands into fists and beat on the pane of Mom's window once, twice, three, four times.

"Lin-da!"

Remember when we were first married and she asked you to call her "Mom?" You've still never done it – not even in the days before she cheerfully and accidentally called you a prostitute for only giving me three children in nine years of marriage. Luckily, by the time she said it, I'd already convinced you Mom never meant any harm, and it was best just to keep laughing at her. We laughed, all right.

I'm pretending not to see her grouchy neighbour as I beckon to you, trying to get you to step out of the flowerbed. "Come out of there. Before someone calls the police."

You jab the glass with your index finger hard enough for me to hear the click of your fingernail. "Maybe we should be the ones calling the police and they can come smash in this window themselves. She's in there," you say before you bend over and try to fluff up the trampled, watery goutweed.

But there's no need to call anyone. Mom's landlord is already standing in the gravel driveway, locking the doors of his pickup truck with his remote control key fob. He's come wearing faded green scrubs like doctors wear in hospitals. Only he's not a doctor. He's a veterinarian who dresses like one on days when he's working indoors, in his surgery. Aunt Marla says he owns most of the trailers here plus a bunch of other shabby little houses all over town. I guess even a tiny community like this one needs a slumlord.

From above his big yellow moustache, he looks down at you where you're still standing in his flowerbed. But he's talking to me. "Sorry about the wait. I had to finish up at my day job."

And that's when the guilt makes its first lunge at me – like maybe I shouldn't have just stood here in the yard all this time, waiting for him to stitch up his last freshly sterilized cat belly of the day. Maybe I should have let you ram your fists through the window – or pushed right past you and crashed into the trailer myself – just to show them all that this matters.

The veterinarian slumlord calls me back as I start up the flaky wooden stairs, up into the shadow of Mom's veranda. "Hey. Since I've got the key and everything, maybe you want me to go in first."

He's holding some kind of skeleton key between two fingers, away from the rest of the bristling mass of metal keys in his palm – like it's a scalpel, or something. And I'm staring into that hospital green he's wearing – a colour I recognize from the spectrum of disaster. You're standing behind him, on the driveway, with your throat flushed red.

I'm agreeing with him. "Oh. Yeah." I punctuate it with a small, phony laugh, for some reason.

The landlord steps around me, in front of me, shorter than me, especially with his head bent low and his shoulders rounded as he digs at the lock with the skeleton key. You're behind me, your hand – hot from all your new pregnancy blood – pressed into the centre of my back.

The door opens and we each yell a "Linda" into the quiet, filthy home of a woman blind on years and years of diabetes

4

denial. I walk into the bedroom where I figure she's mostly likely to be, sick in bed. The landlord moves toward the living room even though there's no sound coming from the television. And you step inside to stand on the grimy tiles between the front door and the bathroom. I hear you sniff at what the sealed windows and the old tobacco residue have kept hidden from us until now.

The smell in here – is it dirty laundry, a stagnant toilet that needs flushing, or fifty-five years of bad breath let out in a great and terrible exhale?

They are wrong when they tell you how it will be when you find the body. Everyone who has tried to imagine it but does not yet know – they are all wrong. They are wrong when they say the smell will be like nothing else. They are wrong. Because even a dead person still smells like a person.

"There she is."

I turn to see the veterinarian trotting out of the living room – head down, shoulders pulled up toward his ears, reigning in the urge to run. And behind him, laid out on the nylon carpet, we see a scruffy grey-brown wig and a set of cheap clothes stained all over with chokecherry syrup. The veterinarian landlord is herding us backward, out the narrow entryway, back onto the veranda. He's not intimidated by an animal as large as me and without having to touch me, he forces me back against your small, hot hand.

"Yup," he says as he pulls the front door closed behind himself, "She's dead."

Even after all this it still feels like a mistake. I'm arguing. "Are you sure?"

Behind me, you're saying my name in a little girl's voice. "Brigs..."

The veterinarian ducks his head like he's reading his watch, and I can hear the gag in his voice as he tells me, "Yes."

In the morning, you're not just sad. You're ashamed. "I woke up in the middle of night and got – all freaked out and scared, like an idiot."

It is stupid, and it's too bad. But I know exactly what you mean. Our loved one has become a Halloween prop, and the grief of it feels differently in our hands than it looks in art or on the news or anywhere else.

The veterinarian landlord had dialled 9-1-1 on his cell phone and urged us not just out the door of the trailer but all the way back up the street to my Aunt Marla's house. That's where our kids and our suitcases and the long, hard task of telling and telling and telling were all waiting for us.

We were well away from the trailer park when the police and the ambulance arrived with a stretcher and a long, zippered bag. It was bad. Mom's body had been there, face down – not awake and not asleep – on the floor in front of her television long enough for her skin to break down, becoming an osmotic membrane. No matter what she used to tell people when she was selling those detoxifying foot pads from that shady herbal health distributor, only corpses have osmotic skin that can drain vital fluids directly into the outside world like a wrung out sponge. Everything inside her had been seeping out into the carpet underneath her body for what must have been days and days.

You talk to the veterinarian on the phone the morning after

they take Mom's body away. He tells you he cut the worst bit of the carpet right up off the floor, hauled it to the dump with a can of gasoline, and lit the whole thing on fire. It was bad. You thank him.

One of the police officers, the vet can't help but tell you, was sick right in the potentilla bush planted at the base of the veranda. After that, the poor cop had to go sit – all humiliated and waiting – in the car. You thank the vet for that too. Mom would have enjoyed it. She never liked the cops.

And you never liked this town – the place where I was raised, the place with generations of my ancestors buried in the cemetery. "They're all talking about it now," you say as we walk back up the block, between the sad, small houses Mom used to call "pokey." We've made the necessary obeisance to our children, updated Aunt Marla, and now we're heading back to the Mountain View Mobile Home Community to clear out the trailer.

"This is the kind of town," you warn me, "where we can never come again without being known as 'the ones who found the body.'"

The medical examiner has already called from the quiet of the Calgary morgue to ask me questions about Mom's medical history. I really don't know much. Mom mostly just bickered with her doctors about the "corporate medical machine," so the information we got was never very good.

When Mom's dead-person doctor heard about her decades of diabetes and the open heart surgery and everything, she told me right away that there won't be any need for a full-blown autopsy. If we want them to give us a toxicology report we'll have to pay them ninety dollars and wait the better part of a year. For the doctor and the woozy policemen, the investigation of my mother's death is finished.

You and I are outside the trailer again. The veterinarian slumlord has left the front door unlocked and all the windows are slid wide open. The rooms are breathing out that warm, gummy stench through the folds of the pleated skirt blinds. After the wrestle with the flaming carpet, the vet has no more pity left for us. He tells us the trailer needs to be completely cleared in the next two days so it can be gutted and scorched and recovered for the use of future renters — as if this town will ever forget to keep calling this place "The Dead Lady Trailer."

You wouldn't let me come back here alone. We leave our kids at Aunt Marla's house for a little longer while we pile Mom's books, bath towels, clothes, dishes, uneaten groceries, and old bits of yellowed computer hardware on the lawn like specimens at an archaeological dig.

The carpet and its foam underlayment are hacked away, leaving a bare, ragged rectangle on the living room floor. It's not quite like one of those crime scene chalk-outline drawings, but it's close. For the first few hours we spend inside in the trailer, we walk around the outline, reverent and ginger. But by the time we leave at the end of the day we've learned to stomp right over it, as if its edges weren't lightly streaked with dried, burgundy blood.

Outside, the neighbours are nowhere. "Look, it's turned into a ghost town out here," you say. "Get it, Brigs — ghost town?"

"Good one. Ya kill me."

And you hold your stomach and laugh way too loudly,

flaunting our presence to all these closed doors and windows.

I don't ask you how you can bear the smell inside the trailer and why you're not sick this morning like you've been every day for the last seven weeks. Maybe it's some kind of evolutionary gift – an extraordinary override your parasympathetic nervous system accepts when it senses its own dead.

"I think I've figured out what happened," you finally tell me. And you walk through the trailer narrating the story in the physical evidence, like a voice-over at the end of one of those Agatha Christie movies Mom used to watch on Sunday nights.

"She's sitting here, having a meal." You stand beside the small kitchen table piled high with pulpy novels and knitting magazines, pointing out the half-eaten grilled cheese sandwich tipping off the edge of a saucer. Mom's primly zipped insulin kit sits beside it.

"And then she's sick." You show me the splotch dried on the linoleum under the table. "So she gets herself to the bathroom."

I follow you.

"And she's – sick again." The small, windowless room is filthy. Mom's clothes lay empty in the hall, still curved around her missing shape, her hollowed pant-legs formed into something like the sign for infinity. It's as if she's been snatched up by the Rapture – one of those Bible words with a headlong Evangelical flair that always makes me kind of nervous. Above the empty clothing, prints of a knee – or maybe the heel of a hand – mark the wall just a few feet off the floor.

"Then she moves along this wall to the bedroom and manages to put on a set of clean clothes, like she's getting ready to go find some help. Next, she must have come into the living room, looking for her purse, or whatever. But she takes a minute to lie down on the rug, maybe just to try to catch her breath, or something. And she doesn't get up."

You're right. Of course you're right.

We work all day, in and out of the trailer, up and down the wooden steps. Before long, the dead smell is in our clothes. It's on our skin and hair and clinging in a film to the moisture on the surfaces of our lips. We can't tell for sure, but it must be stuck to our eyes too.

Yellow-jacket wasps are gathering outside, crawling over the artefacts stacked on the lawn, feeling for what's left of her between the rubber buttons of the remote controls with their twitching black antennae, like little angry Valkyries.

Near the end, when the wind comes up, and it starts to get dark, and even the wasps abandon us, you're standing on the grass with one of the drawers pulled out of the bedroom dresser tipped over at your feet. And you've got her coral pink sweater – the only one she owned that isn't all covered in those fuzzy acrylic pills – clenched in both your hands. It was her favourite. It's been in the family even longer than you've been with us. And I didn't know until right now that when I see my mother in my memory, that sweater is always what she's wearing.

Something like it must be true for your memory too. "Brigs, look." You say it like you're hurt – like you're hurt so badly you can hardly stand it. "How could she not have died in it? And what are we supposed to do with it now?"

I see the sweater, left behind in this world, somehow. It's no heirloom – nothing here is. We can't keep it – not with that smell tangled between all its tiny fibres. I look away from where my wife stands with my mother's second skin pulled taut over her knuckles. But there's nowhere I can turn where I don't see the rest of my mother strewn all over the yard in heaps of reeking ruins.

The funeral director stops short in the glossy, walnut-trimmed doorway. He's every bit as tall and white-haired as an angel from the Book of Revelation, but something about the sight of you and me has startled him. He still has one foot outside the windowless basement vault called the "Family Consultation Room" when he says, "A little young to be down here, aren't you?"

My phony laugh comes back, making you wince toward the tabletop.

The funeral man himself looks like he's about Mom's age. And he's reluctant to accept my order to cremate her body. But then I remember that she once requested it in writing in a legal will made defunct by her remarriages. I move to show him, sliding the old will out of a big manila envelope I've been keeping sealed inside one of those locking plastic bags. The smell of it shouldn't bother a guy like him too much. Actually, I think it may be what finally gets him to start filling out the paperwork.

The sunny little boy we call Levi bangs his head against the bottom of the table again. You've had enough and you're pulling him out by his thin white arms. He doesn't like anything about the wine-coloured quiet of the consultation room. The darkly plush showroom full of urns and caskets is no better for him. The funeral people give him a hard candy and one of their special sorry-for-your-loss stuffed toys, but Levi would rather comfort himself from the horror of his boredom by walking through the showroom smudging his little fingerprints all over the shiny, hot-lacquered finishes of the coffins.

We manage to laugh at the fifteen thousand dollar copper coffin that looks like an escape pod from a science fiction movie. The urns are in an area by themselves — ceramic replicas of Ming vases, metallic capsules that look like they're meant for mixing cocktails. And then we find it: a mahogany case about the size and shape of a jewellery box out of the Sears Christmas catalogue. That's what we order.

"If you want to visit with your mother — before," funeral man begins, "I think I should tell you —"

"No, we're good. We've seen enough," I interrupt.

He's nodding. "That's just fine. Sometimes people have strong ideas about 'closure' but it's certainly not necessary in every case — and it's downright unfortunate in others. Oh, by the by, the husband's already been here to see the deceased."

I know he doesn't mean Dad. I hate that I need to ask him to make his comment more specific. "What did he say his name was?" I ask.

The funeral man tells me the name. It's the Monster-man — the one Mom lived with for two-and-a-half weeks before she had the police come take him away. Ever since she walked out on Dad five years ago, you've been calling Mom a serial marryer. But you never say it in front of Dad. It'd bring on his sigh and his, "She's a romantic." I kind of like the way it hurts me to hear Dad making her excuses. I kind of like the way he tells us, "In her way, she was always a romantic."

Monster-man is the latest in her series of post-Dad marriages — and the final one, I guess. I met him once. It was at their wedding. She wore white every time. As far as the state knows, Monster-man is still my legal stepfather. It means he got to come gawk at her body and then walk out of the funeral home with an application for a government widower's pension.

When we're finished at the funeral home, you start the run-around of ordering the funeral flowers and the food. And I make the rounds with a big folder full of unpaid bills and over-drawn bank statements to show the ex-husbands, in case any of them still believes those stories she used to tell about being on the verge of a million-dollar pyramid sales breakthrough.

When I get to Monster-man, he's bawling like some kind of grizzled, aging reptile on the steps of his social housing com-plex. He's grabbing at me and trying to get me to step through the screen door so we can – I don't know – comfort each other with a bunch of nostalgic slander about her.

"I went to the funeral home."

"Yeah, they told us."

"You should have seen her–"

My voice is dry and – I hope – decisive. "We did."

That's when he offers me the rest of a half-used blister pack of erectile dysfunction tablets. "You know, my heart condition was every bit as bad as hers ever was. And she cared just as little about me having a heart attack as she did about having another one herself." He pushes the sheet of pills against my chest. "Se-riously, man, get these out of here. I don't know how she got her hands on them but she could have killed me, feeding them to me the way she did."

By the time I remember to call the social worker and the probation officer, they've already seen her obituary in the newspaper. I wish I didn't notice the way they sounded almost happy for me – like I'm suddenly and unexpectedly off the hook, or something.

Another wakeful night goes by on the sofa bed in Aunt Marla's rec room, and then it's the morning of the funeral. I guess we still haven't slowed down enough to properly explain what's happening to our own kids. I'm leaning over the bathroom sink trying to hold my necktie out of the way as I spit out mouthfuls of toothpaste when I hear Scottie, our oldest son, ask you, "What *is* a funeral?"

You only pause for a split second before you answer. "It's kind of like a wedding reception – only the bride has to be a dead person."

For now, that's good enough.

At the service, it's you who gives the eulogy. You've been in the family for ten years now, but the American relatives still don't know you very well, and they're worried and unsure what to expect when – small, sleep-deprived, secretly pregnant – you stand up at the pulpit and speak on their behalf. It seems like the whole town gathers to hear how we'll spin her story – chronicle all the mental illness, physical disease, false starts, hurt feelings, squandered money, wasted time – now that it's over. At the end, when you read that bit about "the lilies of the field," everyone's shoulders heave, almost in unison, and we understand that none of us is going to be angry with her forever.

Tomorrow, you'll step out of the nine-foot-tall funeral home doors with a blue velvet bag held horizontally in your hands. I'll be watching from the curb, inside the car where our drowsy little boys will be strapped and bolted into their safety restraints.

"I just realized something," you'll say as you twist into your seatbelt. "I think I was a pall bearer just now."

I'll nod. "Definitely."

My ashes and bone meal mother will be in the velvet bag, in the mahogany box, in the trunk of our Honda-cum-hearse bound for the sprawling, yellow-green, big city cemetery two hundred kilometres away. It's called "The Garden of the Holy Martyrs" with that headlong Catholic flair that always makes me kind of nervous.

When we get there, we'll find the posthole they've dug for her grave – round and bored only three feet down instead of six. I'll use my own bare hands to plant her in the earth, lowering the box in the velvet bag on the end of a gold cord a lot like the one your mother uses to hold back her living room drapes all day long. Then someone will pray before we all just walk away, leaving her there for the invisible groundskeepers to finish her burial.

"You know, Brigs," you'll tell me as I steer our no-longer-a-hearse car onto the township road that will lead us back to the living world, "the next time we go to a funeral, we're just going as guests, okay? We'll come and cry, eat everything we can off the deli trays, and then – we'll leave."

And I'll agree with you even though we both know it's not true. The next time it will all be just the same as it is now. You and I will be the ones left standing forward as the rest of the line falls back. It will always be you and me – banging on the windows, stepping over the bloodstains, mouthing the apologies, paying the cheque, giving the body to be burned.

# Two

Now you're trying to convince me to be cremated too.

"It was so elegant," you insist. "You can't have forgotten that. Everything paper dry, no more than five pounds left by the end, all sealed up in a pretty jewellery box. Your body doesn't even really catch fire during the process. It's more like going into a super-dehydrator than an incinerator. That was what they said, anyways. Remember when they said that, at the funeral home? I mean, dust to dust, right?"

You're adamant that your body is never going to rot. I guess that's fine for you. It's the part about me jumping on the pyre along with you that's still unresolved for me. I don't know where you got it, but you've seized the idea that we both need to dispatch our bodies in exactly the same way – slipping into the Spirit World perfectly matched like a Baby Boomer couple dressed in twin anoraks, tapping squash rinds at a Farmers' Market. I can't quite agree to matching cremations yet. Someone told me once that cremating a body is a desecration of it, and I still haven't decided if it's true.

You're lifting your head from my chest and making that

scoffing sound. "How was what was happening to your Mom's body before we cremated it anything less than utter desecration?"

I let a long breath out my nose. "I know how it looked, but maybe it wasn't really so bad in the big scheme of things. Maybe it just seemed irreverent to us because she started breaking down outside the usual, accepted context—"

"Above ground, below ground, in a box, or out – letting a body rot away is an abomination, Brigs. And I can't imagine there are very many people around here who know that better than you and me."

We're lying in the creaky old bed you bought us the week before we got married, ten winters ago. You paid for it with the money you earned working at the gift-wrap counter at the mall during the Christmas holidays. That was a long time ago. Tonight, the few non-childrearing, non-sleeping hours we get to ourselves every day are almost over. In the quiet and the dimness, you're pressed against me so closely that I don't have much of a sense of the form or texture of your body anymore – only its heat.

Even though you're not quite a full year younger than me, neither of us doubts for an instant that you will outlive me. Maybe it's based on nothing more intuitive than the fact that I'm the male in this marriage. But somehow, we both know that eventually you will be left alone with the two-hundred-pound unanswered question of my corpse.

"So – there is one more deathly thing we need to talk about," you're saying now. When you move against me to look up at my face, I can discern your shape again – yours and a trace

17

of the baby's too. The tips of your fingers lightly press the top of my hand, tracing the bones beneath the skin and veins. My hand-bones spread out in rays, spanning the distance between my wrist and knuckles.

"I wish I knew what it would take to get one of these bones out of your hand after you're dead – before I put you in the furnace," you say. "These bones here – they're the perfect size for keeping..."

I laugh and tell you I don't think it would be legal – something I've heard mentioned in crime stories on the radio about "offering an indignity to a dead body." I think it's an indictable offence and everything.

You're getting angry, dropping my hand onto my chest, leaning away to prop yourself up on your own elbow. "So the state will take your dead body, cut it just about in half to let a stranger help himself to, like, your entire liver, or whatever. But it wouldn't give your own wife one little bone out of your hand? Not even if you wrote instructions for it in your will?"

I don't know, of course. How could I? I fold my hand into a fist and raise it in front of my face where I can see its outline in the near-dark of the northern summer's all-night twilight. You've always had a – thing – about my hands. You call them the perfect archetypal male hands.

"They're like the ones drawn in old anatomy textbooks or in art classes or in religious kitsch," you'd say.

"They just look like regular hands to me," is what I'd say.

And then you'd roll your eyes and tell me, "That is exactly what I mean."

Knowing your fetish for my hands, maybe I should have

expected to hear something like this from you all along. I open my palm and find the back of your head where you've lain down again with your ear on my ribs.

"Your heart always beats so slowly in there," you say, not mad anymore. "It must be humungous."

All your yellow hair is draped over my chest like a spider's web. You haven't bleached any of those trendy white streaks into it – the ones you've started referring to as "turn-of-the-century skunk-hair," as if they're already dated. I don't really care what colour your hair is as long as you don't cut it too short.

Remember that total stranger who rounded on you in the lineup at the grocery store to tell you how selfish it was to keep your hair long while you had little babies in the house? She said she'd heard of a baby once who got a piece of long hair wrapped around his pudgy finger so tightly and for so long that the whole thing had to be amputated. Poor little guy couldn't even remember having that finger. Sure, it's a sad story – if it ever really happened – but I just comb my fingers down the length of your hair and hope for the best.

Should I ask you why you're afraid you won't be able to love me anymore after I've gone all dead and abstract? Is that why you want to take something concrete out of my body to keep with you until you're dead and abstract yourself? But I know you'd just answer me with one of our favourite eschato-logical maxims about how it takes a spirit and a body to make a soul. Lots of people try to believe it, I guess. But you know it's true. Instead, I ask, "What would you do with one of my hand-bones anyway?"

"I told you what I'd do with it," you say. "I'd keep it – just keep it." You promise to treat any bone cut from my hand with careful reverence, insisting you wouldn't use it for anything grisly. "I wouldn't even let anyone else know I had it. And it wouldn't be left out with the living forever. There'd be a secret addendum in my will leaving instructions for the boys to bury it with me."

"You mean, instructions to have it burned up with you."

"Right, right."

While you live, you promise, my hand-bone would stay hidden, tied around your neck as a token of my life, dangling inside your clothes – clean and white in a secret reliquary, hung low on your breast.

I still don't know.

And there's no way to resolve any of it tonight, so I start to fall asleep. I wish you could sleep lying across my chest. But you can't, so you pull away from me. You're rolling over to sleep on your back beneath the high, taut dome of your womb. You told me once that the baby feels like a sack of ball bearings rolling and spilling inside your guts. It's not something I like to think about too much.

I'm not afraid to see you sleeping on your back, even though the ever-shifting gnosis of the pregnancy books stashed under our bed tells us a sleeping position like that one is anathema. But there it is – sleeping on your back, growing all that hair, burying a husband with his skeleton intact – I guess there's always some kind of risk to be taken.

# Three

Still alive, the first of your grandfathers to die comes lurching toward the light in the doorway over his head. He bends, ducking beneath the slope of the ceiling's low overhang much too soon, climbing the stairway out of his basement, hunched low enough for his fingers to graze the tops of the grey wooden stairs. A rebuilt washing machine motor sits on a sheet of two-year-old newspaper on the cement floor below. Today, his fingers are stiff and faraway, unfit for grappling inside something as dim and close and greasy as the washing machine's innards.

In the narrow basement doorway, he slumps at the edge of your grandmother's sunlit kitchen. His left arm rises in front of his face, lifted against the hard sting of noontime glaring through the window. Beyond the bright squares of sunlight falling onto the dark yellow floor, a little woman stands slicing potatoes into a battered aluminum pot.

Sometimes, when I'd come into a room too fast at a family reunion, when I was looking at something else but I could see her in the periphery, I might think your grandmother was you – hardly five feet tall with a cranium I could palm like a softball and that skeleton built almost like a little boy's but definitely not like a little boy's. She's your grandmother, all right. Anyone could tell.

You make the same kind of mistake sometimes too. Remember the last time my family got together for a picnic – the time you came up behind my brother and clamped your arms around his waist before you realized he wasn't me? I can still see him, dark eyebrows arched high, holding your wrists at arm's length while you strained against him. You were screaming and cackling and trying to explain yourself.

But you're not quite a part of this chapter of the story yet. Right now, you're fifteen years old, sleeping through your summer holidays in a perpetually unfinished bedroom without a door, in a corner of your parents' basement. You're nowhere near the house where your grandfather starts to die over a broken washing machine. He is about to become the first dead person you've ever known – just like your mother always promised you.

Your grandfather still doesn't know for certain what's begun as he stands in the kitchen facing the back of your grandmother's blouse. It's a white field muddied with a print of large, brown flowers like no one ever sees growing anywhere in real life.

"Dinner won't be ready for a while," she says to him without turning. Water sloshes in the pot, displaced by the back-yard-grown vegetables.

He steps into the kitchen, his right leg frozen like it's asleep, still standing sheathed in polyester trousers, stretching long and distant all the way to the rubber shoe sole that grips the floor under his foot. The leg lumbers beneath him, snagging on the surface of the yellow floor.

Passing from the kitchen into the living room, he reaches

out for the back of his armchair – the one he brought home strapped to the vinyl top of his Chevy Impala, the five-dollar garage-sale price tag still pinned to the cushion. The pads of his fingers are just as numb as his leg now, telling him nothing about the familiar, nubby texture of the low, nylon loops in the chair's fabric. The hand doesn't grip. It rolls against the coarse brown upholstery like a waterlogged, empty glove.

He jerks and lets his body fall sideways, into the seat of the armchair. A chord of creaks and moans sounds out from the old springs and wood inside it. Maybe he looks up at the wooden sunburst clock hanging on the wall, clicking like a metronome. Or maybe he just sees the clock in his memory.

The outline of a dull headache is reshaping itself, changing out of its fuzzy, formless mass, stiffening into something rigid – its edges becoming defined, tightening into sharper and sharper contrast. The ache hardens into a knife of stunning pain inside his head. The blade draws back, pauses, and stabs deeply into his brain. White light flashes, moving forward through his skull to the backs of his eyes. And then it's dark – like he's suddenly fallen to sleep.

His mouth opens to call for your grandmother, but the sound he makes is nothing like her name. Her paring knife clatters onto the stovetop, as if she already knows what it all means. She's moving in the dark spaces around his body, small and somewhere beyond him.

"I'm callin' the ambulance," she says. Her feet carry her back into the kitchen with a hard, staccato sound, like a volley of darts fired into the floor. And she's out of his reach.

"Shoes," he remembers. "Even in the house it was always shoes with us."

He sits. He knows the upholstery on the chair's back is still sagging against his weight. He can feel it through the darkness and the numbness. And he still knows the smell on his skin is the washing machine's white grease. There is still clarity in the sound and meaning of your grandmother's words as she speaks into the enormous green rotary telephone hung on the kitchen wall.

"He's tryin' to talk, and I can't understand him at all. I think he's in real trouble."

The heavy telephone receiver lands in its metal hook. There's a grind and click as your grandmother twists a dial on the stove and abandons her cooking. And that's when he knows he won't ever eat again. What comes next is – nothing. He loses the sonic tie that links him to his wife's voice and feet. In the quiet, he's set adrift, dark and silent.

Bracing himself against the horror of the language-less sound, he tries to call to her again.

There's another flurry of darts on the floor before they're muffled on the shabby carpet in front of him. She's standing over his armchair. "They say they're coming quick as they can. I'm just in the bedroom packing a few things in case it turns out…"

As she speaks, he sweeps his last strong arm like a scythe out into the darkness where he knows she hovers. He reaps her off her feet and into the armchair, on top of his body. She falls, tangling with him.

"Settle down. There's nothing we can do but wait. They're coming…"

She's sitting up, getting away, but he finds her waist before she can properly rise, and gathers her, folded at her middle, into his lap. His live hand gropes for her head, combing through the wiry grey hair at the nape of her neck, closing around the narrow base of her skull. He pulls her head under his chin. She gives in, gets quiet, and he breathes in the scent of her crown – all deep and greedy – like it's forgiveness itself.

And then the metallic clasps and hinges are rattling like bear claws scraping at the front door. She's gone, quick as Goldilocks. He feels other hands on him now, deftly pulling his body out of its armchair and down onto a carpeted floor. It's clean but at close range the carpet smells grey – like dust and melted snow. There are paws and growls all around him now. And there's a new draft wafting in like the Spirit World through the open screen door.

The dying drags on for days and days. Again, everything is just like your Mom promised you it would be. It lasts long enough for everyone in your family to fall all the way down into the very lowest hollows of what I guess we could call the valley of the shadow of death, or whatever.

For your mother, the fall to the lowest point in her grief happens in the grocery store in your grandmother's small town. The store manager hasn't heard that your grandfather is still animated by the ventilator tube in his throat. Maybe that's why he walks right up to your mother in the dairy department and offers to start the cold cut order for the funeral lunch.

Your Dad's low point is that fight he has with your Uncle Terry in the waiting room of the intensive care unit in the city hospital. It happens right out in the open – by the vending machines, next to the elevators – where anybody could see and hear them. Even though your Dad swears he never said anything to get him started, your Uncle Terry points his finger right under your Dad's collar bone and starts to whisper-yell, all heady with grief.

"You think I did this. You think this is a chiropractic-induced stroke. You always loved a good witch hunt, didn't you, Frank?"

But your Dad just opens his hands and raises them both in front of himself, like an unarmed cowboy in a dusty brown movie with a soundtrack that's nothing but whistling and reverb.

Your other uncle – Ned – he lunges between them with the barrier of his rumpled pinstriped business suit and his special status as their baby brother. He's on his feet for the first time since he arrived here from the Calgary office tower where he works seventy hours a week doing – no one's completely sure what. Until now, he's been slumped in a yellow vinyl waiting room chair, quietly tearing an empty Styrofoam cup into a long, curled ribbon, almost as if he's peeling a Christmas orange. It's like a game he used to play when he was a kid. When the game went well, he would come running to his mother brandishing a long, pungent strand of thin orange peel in his sticky white hands.

He'd wave the rind right in her face. "I peeled the whole thing without breaking it!"

"Did ya? Now throw the peel over your shoulder," his mother would answer. "The letter it makes when it hits the ground is the first letter in the name of the girl you're gonna marry someday."

"Hey guys, I've been thinking," is what grownup Ned says to interrupt the tension between his brothers. "Maybe we just need to work with Dad some more." He's talking fast, bobbing his head to break up the dangerous line of sight strung between your Uncle Terry and your Dad. "You know what I mean: play some Mozart CDs in his room, or bring in that nice tame cat they have at home for some – what would you call it – tactile therapy, or read him some really good poetry."

Your Dad steps back, happy to be dropping his surrendering cowboy pose. "The old man's having a stroke, Ned, not giving us the silent treatment. I don't think all that 'rage, rage against the dying of the light' stuff is going to help us much anymore."

But Uncle Terry isn't finished with your Dad yet. He raises his hand to Ned's chest and presses against his sternum until Ned moves out of his view of your father's face. "Not that it has *anything* to do with this, Frank," Uncle Terry says, "but I never, ever laid a hand on the old man's neck – never."

It's late in the evening when Uncle Terry stands outside the hospital waiting area, right in front of the open door of your grandfather's room. He's talking with a doctor who has never introduced himself to any of them, which is just about proof positive that this doctor must be the person in charge here. The folded ribbon of paper marked with flat-lines drawn by the stylus of the hospital's EEG machine is clipped to the board the doctor holds in his hand.

In the domain of his own hospital ward, the doctor seldom whispers anything, not even when it comes to death. "It's not that the manual tests for assessing what you'd call brain death aren't perfectly humane," he's telling your Uncle Terry. "They certainly are. However, the tests tend to elicit quite a bit of – anxiety in family members who see them applied."

Uncle Terry hisses something in return.

The doctor makes one clipped nod over the stiff collar of

his shirt. He isn't dressed in the same wrinkly green pyjama-scrubs as the rest of the hospital people. Instead, he's dressed like a lawyer, only with a white lab coat over his shirt and tie – like the kind of doctor who looks right into the camera and recommends a cough medicine in a television commercial.

"Of course," he answers Uncle Terry. "Of course, there's nothing the hospital can do to prevent you from being present when we run through the tests but –. In order to properly establish what you'd call brain death, we need to push the nervous system toward certain limits. And since the nervous system is really just an incredibly intricate bio-electrical machine, it is possible for it to – misfire. The body can mimic signs of life even though it's no longer alive in a meaningful way."

"You're saying he might twitch or something when you go and scrub the Q-tip over his corneas? Because I read about that and I think I'm–"

The doctor is finally whispering as he interrupts Uncle Terry now. "There's a neurological phenomenon called the Lazarus Sign Reflex. Have you read about that?"

"No."

"Well, sometimes bodies of people in what you'd call brain death can momentarily lift their own arms and drop them onto their chests." The doctor bends his arms at the elbows and crosses his wrists over his chest. He holds the pose for a moment, as if he's pretending to be a cartoon Egyptian mummy folded up in its sarcophagus – a mummy buried holding a clipboard. He lets his arms fall to his sides as he begins to speak again. "Naturally, the Lazarus Sign is very striking. When it happens, it can truly appear as if the body is reanimating, and it can be – confusing for the family. But, of course, it's just a simple reflex arc in the spine at work, nothing more."

The spine – all this time, it really was all about the spine.

The doctor closes a hand around your Uncle Terry's shoulder and shakes him gently. Terry's arm rolls in its socket as the doctor speaks. "Listen, no matter what anyone sees hereafter, your father's death is imminent. It's like I told your mother just now. We see from the EEG that his brain no longer functions at all. And his heart and lungs are only continuing to work because of the hospital's life support equipment."

Uncle Terry's eyes glaze over a little bit, remembering a zoology laboratory in his first year of university where he and the other undergraduate science students skinned the legs of frogs who'd been freshly killed ("sacrificed" – in science we say "sacrificed"). The students jabbed tiny electrodes into the large nerves in the thigh muscles and then stood at their lab benches taking turns connecting the electrodes to battery packs, watching the wet, pink flexion of the muscles in the flayed legs. Maybe it's just this memory that makes him feel like he can smell formalin fumes blowing over his face through the hospital's ventilation ducts.

"Look," the doctor says. "I wouldn't say the Lazarus Sign Reflex happens often. But when it does it's a very difficult thing for family members to witness. So most families prefer to let us carry on the testing without them."

The glaze over your Uncle Terry's eyes hardens and clouds until he can barely see at all.

"We're going to proceed now," the doctor says. He's not talking to Uncle Terry anymore, but to the little throng of people in green who've been collecting outside your grandfather's room. A nurse is tugging at the curtain hung from the ceiling, drawing it around the bed where a machine breathes into your grandfather's body as he, or something like him, lies tucked beneath a stiff yellow sheet.

Uncle Terry turns his head to look at the drawn curtain now standing between himself and his father. The doctor's clear, unhushed voice is sounding on the other side of the fabric – narrating everything for the benefit of the medical students being initiated into the secret society of medically managed death. Your uncle's thick fingers are reaching out, moving toward the edge of the curtain. It's woven just barely too densely to be sheer, and it seems to drift away from his hand, pushed on some kind of invisible current in the dry, antiseptically cool air. His fingers graze the cloth, but his hand snaps back at the touch, closing into a fist. He clamps his eyes shut, gritting his teeth, desperate, hoarse as he's whispering.

"Come forth."

You stumble into the darkest chasm of your grief for your grandfather on the same night the hospital people take their ventilator away from him – after the room fills up with doctors and residents pouring cold water inside his ears and pricking at his skin to make sure he's really gone. The round of tests is the last thing the medical people will do for him before they shut off the machines, push back the curtain, and call the adults of your family into the room to watch your grandfather finish his medically delayed dying.

But you don't see any of that. You don't even hear about

it until hours after you've gone to bed in that unfinished basement, your eyes open in the darkness. There's just enough light
in your room to make the joists and wires in the ceiling look
like their images are made of flickering grey pixels, dimly lit
over your head.

Your mother has already come down the stairs, looking
through the dark house for someone awake – someone she
could tell what happened to her father-in-law. She hung up the
telephone after the final call from the hospital, left her bed, and
came through the space in your bedroom wall where a door has
never been hung. She didn't turn on a light as she stood there
and told you the coma – an embarrassing word twitching with
histrionic TV silliness – had ended. And now your grandfather
isn't just brain dead, he's truly dead.

Even after days of hearing unfortunate phrases like "vegeta-
tive state," you're still kind of shocked at the news. Shock isn't
a complicated sensation. You know you are shocked. What you
aren't sure of yet is whether you feel sad.

The truth is your grandfather never took much notice of
you – the mess of blonde hair sitting there on the ottoman beside his feet while the hockey game wheeled round and round
on the white screen between the beer commercials. No matter
how many times you asked him to explain the rules of offside,
he would always start by saying, "Well, first of all, you aren't
allowed to get ahead of the play."

And then you'd wait at least three beats before you'd say,
"Granddad, what does it mean to get ahead of the play?"

You recognize another feeling. It's confusion. You don't
know how to craft a proper sorrow of your own. You're not

even really sure what it is you're missing – what's at the heart of this unmistakeable but unformed sense of loss. So you try to imagine what your grandmother's grief must be like instead. You try, but it's hard to see how her mood could be much different from the melancholy, recovering-Calvinist temperament the she always seems to have even at picnics and birthday parties. Still, you close your eyes and try to will your mind out across the kilometres of flat farmland between your bed and your grandmother's. Maybe you're caught up in one of those teenaged fantasies about having psychic powers that have been lying dormant, waiting for something like a death in the family to spark them into action.

It's late at night, but the idea that your grandmother is asleep doesn't seem very likely. What does she look like when she sleeps, anyway? In all your years together in the family, you've never seen her asleep. It's not very often that she breaks from her typical, interrupted-squirrel attitude and takes a seat let alone a nap. To you and the other grandkids, she is all flying potato peels and quick, hard footsteps, her arms always cocked at the elbows, held at right angles, ready to spring.

The best you can do is to imagine your grandmother lying under a well-pressed bed sheet with her eyes wide open to the dry, quiet air of her old bungalow. On the bedside table beside her is your grandfather's old-fashioned folding alarm clock – the one with hands that used to glow in the dark before you were born, before their slightly radioactive, blue-green promethium paint with the short, short half-life expired. The clock will be ticking in the dark like a small, frantic heart.

Maybe you know the timber and plaster and furniture of

your grandparents' funny little house better than you know the old people themselves. All those cold white Boxing Day afternoons stuck inside the house with their angel-haired Christmas tree and the turkey soups they ruined by glutting them with boiled barley kernels – those days drove you so deeply into boredom that you learned every mote of your grandparents' house. You turned each bit of it over and over as you looked and looked for something to see.

It was especially true after the visit from the vacuum cleaner salesman with the machine made of the same material as the space shuttle. The vacuum salesman was the first person you ever heard claim that most household dust is actually dead skin sloughed off the bodies of living humans. The dust was your grandparents themselves, chafing against their upholstery while they watched television or read Louis L'Amour novels. You're still not sure you believe him. But your grandparents let the salesman turn his amazing sucking space machine on the couch cushions and on their own bedroom mattress. They watched with frigid tolerance as the stranger dumped small, yellowed hills of dust – their skin – onto black velvet circles. The salesman lined up the dust specimens on the coffee table and motioned at you and your brothers with polite, professional disgust.

"Look at that. You don't want the grandkids playing in *that*, do ya?"

The space shuttle vacuum cost more than any car your grandparents had ever bought, so they kept their complimentary knife set and sent the salesman away. But maybe if they'd let him clean the whole house – every pillow and mattress and bath mat – the coffee table would have been covered in a heap of dead skin as big as both your grandparents put together. It would have been finer than dry, prairie snow – deep, and inextricably blended, a million individual flakes combined so well it doesn't matter anymore if they aren't all exactly alike.

Maybe your grandparents' house seems so singular in your memory just because it was different from the aluminum sided, split level boxes where you and me and all our friends lived out our childhoods. All along its outside surfaces, your grandparents' house is armoured with hard grey stucco bristling with tooth-sized bits of gravel and broken glass coloured green, brown, and white.

Underneath their house, there's a basement that's more like a cellar – an uninhabited concrete box with one wall hidden behind columns of oversized, bare aluminum cans labelled with thick, black letters hand-printed onto their sides.

"Powdered Skim Milk, Elbow Macaroni, Salt."

The cans hold your grandparents' emergency food supply. Your Dad told you they had enough food in those cans to keep themselves alive for an entire year without ever needing to go grocery shopping. If one of those Cold War doomsday bombs had ever dropped out of the sky, your grandparents could have sealed themselves in the bunker of their basement, dry-swallowing dehydrated potato pearls by the light of a hurricane lamp, perching on boxes stuffed with old newspapers and military service medals, observing that this wasn't the first time they've seen the end of the world.

In your bedroom, on the night your grandfather dies, you open your eyes and admit that there must not be any latent ESP hidden inside your brain. It's time to forget your grandmother long enough to make your own way toward grief. You turn over in your narrow girl's bed, trying to call back to your senses the pungent herbal smell that wafts out of your grandfather's bedroom door whenever you walk past it on the way to their bathroom. Your Mom told you the smell was from the tubes of ointment your grandfather massaged into the bone spurs in his knees before he went to bed every night. Its smell rubs off on his sheets, penetrates the mattress as he sleeps, and hangs over the bed like incense while he's gone all through the day.

Sometimes, you and the other grandkids would stand on the threshold of his bedroom – held at bay by the gloom cast over everything by the heavy Black Watch fabric of the drapes that stayed drawn across the window all day long. The curtains were scary, but so was the shallow water glass where you knew his teeth spent the nights. And you'd all stand there on the threshold arguing, trying to decide what familiar smell most perfectly matched the ointment on your grandfather's bed sheets. Everyone used to shout you down whenever you claimed the smell was just like homemade root beer. But you're so convinced that's what it was, you don't even remember what the other kids used to argue in return.

In the pixels on your bedroom ceiling, you are starting to see flashes of deep brown between the greys and blacks. And that's when you know for sure – the ointment did smell like root beer. You know it did. Maybe that is the seat of your kinship with the first dead person you've ever known – the secret of your grandfather's ointment.

It's a fine bond, but you grasp at it, stretching your fingertips up toward the flecks of brown flashing in the ceiling. You even close your fist, as if you're actually holding onto something with your small white hand. And you pull your fist back, toward your chest, holding it tightly enough to squeeze a single, cool tear out of one of your eyes. You stay awake, marking the tear's slow trail out of your eye, across your temple – falling and falling until it fractures into a hundred tiny rivulets, pouring into the delta of your hairline.

# Four

But wait – tonight, in your grownup world where you live with me and our sons in our house in the suburbs, there's something in the newsfeed on your computer screen that makes you choke out a little cry. I can hear you all the way from the kitchen, upstairs. Down in the basement, you're reading a story about the rediscovery of the body of King Ramses the First, founder of the nineteenth dynasty of ancient Egypt – though that's not how you've always known him.

"It's them," you call up the stairs to me. "Brigs, come see."

"Them."

"Yeah. It's those mummies from that daredevil museum in Niagara Falls. I told you about them. Remember?"

And then I do remember that story of yours about the childhood summer vacation when you looked into case after glass display case of desiccated, pillaged human bodies. They were on display in a tourist-trap museum. Your family ended up there after you'd finished watching all you could bear of the Niagara River falling over a cliff in the rain.

Something occurs to me as I follow your voice down the

37

stairs: your mother was wrong. Your grandfather wasn't really the first dead person you'd ever seen. She herself had shown you other corpses, years before you saw his – the mummies, a whole cavalcade of dry brown death. For some reason, she must not have thought of the mummies as truly human – or as truly dead. Before she took you to your grandfather's funeral, your mother had pushed the admission money through a hole in the ticket-seller's glass and brought you to see the world famous mummies of the Niagara Falls Daredevil Museum.

The computer tells us your mummies came to the museum after losing their way and falling among thieves sometime in the nineteenth century. That's how they ended up lying in rows of glass sarcophagi in a carnival-style museum upstream from Lake Erie. And that's where they stayed for years and years, caught in a bad funeral that threatened to go on until the end of the world.

One of the mummies, you tell me, had his wrappings peeled back so the tourists could see his face and his reddish beard. Another one – the one you're calling your favourite – had thick hair, plaited into long braids, and heaped up like a pillow around her head. You say the body that disturbed you the very most was not really a body at all – just an unattached hand and a foot.

"I never thought of it before, but looking back," you tell me now, "I don't know why I assumed that hand and foot belonged to the same person. It wasn't like there was anything in the display to prove that they ever did."

Still, the appendages lay next to each other, under glass, in Canada for over a hundred years. Maybe that was the beginning and the end of their connection. And maybe it was enough.

You don't remember anything in particular about the only mummy mentioned in the news story on the computer today. He's the one found shifted into a mislabelled coffin, resting with his arms crossed high over his chest – just like Tutankhamen and the rest of the desecrated kings. He's the one the archaeologists rescued right out of the "Hall of Freaks" exhibit, years after your visit. They scanned and examined him – centrifuged flakes of his papery skin – until they became almost certain he was truly King Ramses. His fame doesn't make any difference to your memory – you still can't recall a single thing about him.

You just shrug when I question you about King Ramses. "It's because he's completely bald. I was a little girl, remember? At the time, I had been indoctrinated to value everything according to hairdos."

Now, I've crouched down beside your chair at the computer, looking through a disgusted kind of squint at the online mummy photo gallery. Even on the small, flat screen it's pretty ghastly. Over the images of the mummies, I can see my own face reflected in the glare of the screen – dark and ghostly and pinched. "Tell me again how old you were when your parents took you to see these guys in person?"

You do some kind of math on your fingertips before you answer. "Nine."

"And all your younger brothers were there with you?"

"Yup."

"That means Troy would have been…"

"Three years old."

I don't know how the parenting choices our mothers and

fathers made under the influence of the I'm-OK-You're-OK ethos of our childhoods can still surprise me, but sometimes, they do.

"That reminds me." You're turning away from me, back to the light of the screen. "They had a mummified baby exhibited there too. Let's see if we can find him."

But I'm reaching for your hand, knocking it away from where it curves over the computer mouse. "That's enough," I'm saying in my Dad-voice. "You're going to give yourself nightmares again."

"What are you talking about?"

"This is exactly like the time we stayed up late watching that online slide show of the Holy Catholic Incorrupt Saints."

I know you remember those pictures – all those bodies unearthed and dressed up and laid out in shrines at cathedrals and monasteries. The captions on the slide show claimed the bodies of the saints' smell like flowers or honey, and they aren't really rotting. But I can see as well as any pilgrim and – I hate to sound disrespectful but – I don't know, I guess there must be lots of different ways not to rot.

Still, I know you remember Clare of Montefalco with the image of a cross burnt into her heart muscle. And Saint Sylvan with his head thrown back and his throat still slit. And Zita who lies there in her fancy dress without any of the usual wax coverings to obscure the view of how her skin has turned black all over her face and hands. Then there's that saint lying incorrupt in Winnipeg, not quite a thousand miles from here. We could drive there and see his shrine ourselves – even though they admit some of his toes have fallen off by now.

We saw all those pictures of the Incorrupt Saints just hours before you spent the night dreaming nothing but nightmares. We watched their images flick by on this same computer screen in our basement. The slide show was five minutes long, the soundtrack was an Eastern Orthodox funeral chant, and it was almost over by the time you finally turned and asked me, "How in the flaming heck did we come to be looking at this?"

And now that we've found the Saints' heathen cousins in the digital photos of the Niagara Falls mummies, you're shoving me out of the way so you can see them better, pulling the plastic mouse right off the desk so I can't take it away from you. "No, I will not be scared. This is not scary, Brigs. This is different. This is my childhood."

"I know you honestly don't think you'll be scared now, but in a few hours you'll be waking me up doing that thing where you moan out loud in your sleep like a frightened little girl. It freaks me out. And then I have to shake you awake and bring you back and tell you it was just a dream. I hate it. It's too – sad."

You've never heard it yourself – that sound you only make when you're asleep. You don't know it's the worst thing I've ever heard.

So you keep struggling with me, trying to click on the links to rest of the gallery, looking for that mummified baby boy. We tangle until you're on your feet, out of your chair. It falls over, backwards, onto the floor. And you're scream-laughing and making ridiculous threats at me as I grab at you. We're down on the floor and I'm growling with my mouth pressed to the side of your face, hot-breathed and wishing the boys were already in bed.

The boys – they know a crash means a good time and they come running at the sound of the chair clattering onto the hard floor. They're capering, laughing, ready to fight for or against either of us. Scottie, our biggest boy, leads them, of course. He's the first of them to come careening into the basement, advancing with all the noise of someone spilling a bundle of yard tools down the stairs.

There's just an instant left before we know they'll tumble past the turn-around in the staircase and get to where they can see everything – you and me, breathless and flushed, and the mummies, all dry and brown. We're pulling apart now, getting to our feet, rushing against the boys' coming, the both of us standing at the desk again. I plant myself in front of the monitor, moving to block their view so all they'll see will be the back of my T-shirt. You're thrashing at the wires and keys, desperate to shut it all down, to cut the power to this ancient, worn-out kind of death, burnt in bright liquid light across the screen.

## Five

Before you even know you're awake, your eyes are already open in the darkness – like maybe you were sleeping without closing them. What is this place? The light outside the window slants into the room from the wrong direction. There are no grey-brown pixels on the ceiling. Instead there's an orange glow coming from a street lamp outside. You can see it through the floor-length sheers drawn across a large, street-level window. The light outside keeps back the dimness almost well enough for you to be able to read the time marked on the face of the wooden sunburst clock hung on the wall at your feet.

But it's the smell of the room – the pungent, herbal smell seeping from underneath the bedroom door at the end of the hall, out of the mattress inside, like homemade root beer – that finally orients you. And you remember you're in a sleeping bag, on the floor, in the living room of your grandparents' house. You're waiting for the morning to come, when you'll play a role you still don't understand as one of the guests at your grandfather's funeral.

Of course, all of this happens long before our boys are born to teach you how to slam back into wakefulness at the smallest sound. It'll be years before you learn to sleep with your hearing primed and alert. You haven't yet reached the point you live at now, where you're never more than just half asleep. No matter how long I live or how many kids we have it will never be like that for me. There will always be some part of my unconscious mind that hears the little cries in the night and sleeps on and on – fat, loathsome, and fatherly in a way that's more reptile than it is human.

"Hear that crying, Dude?" ugly, unconscious, reptile-dad will always drawl into my sleep. "Sure you do. But it's got nothing to do with us."

Something unusual must be happening in the house where you're staying on the night before your grandfather's funeral – something strange and loud enough to reach you through the tsunami depths of your adolescent sleep waves. You lie awake and listen while your brothers breathe noisily from where they sleep on the living room couches, wrapped in their sleeping bags like plump nylon caterpillars capped with dark, hairy heads. On the floor beside you, bent delicately into a shape like a pretty crescent moon, is your cousin Janae. She's your Uncle Ned's oldest daughter – the only one Aunt Tammy agreed to let him bring to the funeral.

In one sleepy instant, you've remembered all about the funeral. And you're left alert and waiting for the sound that woke you to come again. There it is, sounding from beneath the floorboards. You hear a thud and a kind of grating as something heavy rolls along a cement slab. The grating ends when whatever had been rolling comes to rest against a hollow steel shell with a muted clang. Somebody is in the basement.

You rustle out of the sleeping bag and onto your bare feet. The mucous-y racket of Uncle Ned's snoring blasts from underneath a closed bedroom door. It really is awful. No wonder Aunt Tammy was so quick to throw him out.

Through the kitchen, you can see that the basement door is standing barely ajar. No light shines through the spaces between the door and its jambs. You step onto the linoleum, moving toward the basement door on your bare feet. Isn't that where they said it happened – in the basement? Isn't that where your grandfather started pulling away from the rest of you, beginning the slow drama of his death?

You reach out your hand toward the door, expecting it to creak when it moves, like a prop in a scary movie. But it swivels smoothly on its hinges, opening a black mouth with an oily silence that might be even more horrible than a creak. You imagine that the air the basement breathes up into your face smells like a newly dug grave – though you won't know for sure what that smells like until you go to the cemetery tomorrow. The earthy mustiness is really just the smell of last season's potatoes. They're stored underneath the basement stairs, spread in a single layer like starchy raisins withering and sprouting with white towers toward where sunlight sometimes breaks through the cracks between the treads and the risers.

You stand on the edge of the basement maw, your skin prickling all over, because you know you're a doomed heroine from a Gothic novel. If your grandfather has a ghost, it is in the basement – right now – grinding its bones against the concrete floor in the darkness.

"Hello?" you whisper-call down the stairs.

45

There's another thud and a roll. You're too scared now to keep from flicking on the light switch inside the basement door. Through your squinting, you see a rumpled sleeping bag lying at the foot of the stairs. A pile of shiny tin cylinders – the oversized cans from your grandparents' emergency food storage – still rock gently into one another at the base of the washing machine.

"Granddad?"

There's no voice to answer you. Holding onto the wall, you duck your head in case you've grown tall enough to bang it on the overhang as you step heavily onto the wooden stairs. Below the groaning of the planks under your cold feet, you hear a human sound – panting and a gasp.

"Granddad?"

Opposite the basement machines – the washer, the dryer, the workbench with a power saw under-mounted in its middle – something is collapsed on the floor. It's slumped against the wall of empty shelves that should be stacked with canned food. Whatever it is, you know it's not your grandfather. It sits on the concrete floor holding its right arm in its left hand and rocking back and forth, hissing with shallow breaths.

And then you know it. His ghost – it's your grandmother.

You hurry down the rest of the stairs to crouch beside her. Somehow, you understand it's desperately important to keep quiet. You're young enough to know not to make any vain exclamations or start fussing or demanding an explanation of what she's been doing, alone and hurt in the dark.

Instead, you begin with the whisper of the always inadequate question: "Are you alright?"

Your grandmother can't quite speak but she glances up into your face. At other times, she's noted that your face has always been like your mother's. Only your face is wide open and scared. Your grandmother's own face is shocked pale and slicked with a salty sheet of cold sweat. And if you were a bit older, maybe you wouldn't be able to recognize the specific strain of pain in your grandmother's look. But every kid knows shame when she sees it.

"Grammie?"

Your grandmother doesn't stop rocking herself but she does manage to add voice to the air moving through her teeth. "My arm," she pants. "I fell on it."

You look up to the top of the stairs where the doorway stands dark and gaping. "All the way down the stairs?" you ask.

She shakes her head and jerks it toward the wall of machines. "No. From there."

You follow her gesture with your eyes. Again, you see the khaki army surplus sleeping bag lying as empty as a newly shed snake skin across the feet of the workbench. The table saw is unplugged from the wall outlet, and the saw blade on top of the workbench has been lowered far enough to disappear into the steel surface. A small cushion still rests at one end of the workbench like a pillow lain neatly on a bed. All at once, every bit of the picture becomes clear.

She does sleep, after all. She sleeps there – underground, over the blade, on the narrow, steel deck of the saw table. This is the hard bedrock of her sacrifice.

There's nothing for you to do but to bend over to look at the arm your grandmother clasps against her stomach. You don't remember enough about how her arm usually looks to be able to know if it seems damaged now. "Is it broken?" you ask.

"Don't know."

"I – think you need to go to the hospital," you whisper.

But she doesn't quite hear you. "Hm?"

"The hospital."

She lowers her head over her arm. "Dammit."

From the basement, you creep back up the stairs and go right into the room where Uncle Ned sleeps. Your grandmother has sent you to try to find something for her to wear outside the house. Maybe this night is the first time you've ever moved inside a dark, sleeping house in this particularly feminine state of quiet. It's not new to your grandmother. She knew to promise you that Uncle Ned's snores would cover any noise you make. Your Dad always said it was a shame Ned never got his tonsils out when he was a kid. Now, they say, it's too late.

When you return to the basement, you find your grandmother unmoved from where she'd been sitting on the concrete floor. Her good hand is still clamped around her busted arm, and she makes no move to take the clothing you bring. The pair of you is stalled – waiting for something. Maybe it's for your parents, sleeping in the travel trailer outside in the backyard. There must be some sort of social adaptor that can show you the secret place where you and your grandmother can become properly connected. Even in the fit of this emergency, it still doesn't seem possible that you could have anything truly helpful to offer her. Rescuing her seems incomprehensible – profane, like that Bible story about reaching out a hand to steady a holy relic and being struck dead for it.

Upstairs, Uncle Ned heaves out a massive snore you can both hear from the basement. In unison, you look up at the underside of the floor.

Your grandmother shakes her head, as if she's waking. "Up off the ground," she says.

You wrap an arm around her back. She pulls her feet underneath herself and each of you straightens at the knees, standing up together.

"Over to the stairs," she tells you, inhaling instead of exhaling as she speaks.

You keep hold of her shoulders as she sits down on the grey wood. When you help her slide her nightdress away from her tender arm, the air caught inside the fabric drifts away from her body and into your face. Its smell fills your nose – familiar. It's something like your own smell – musty and feminine – only her scent is shot through with traces of men and work. It smells like the earth of a backyard garden, early in the morning – a garden that's bountiful and beloved but badly tended.

Your grandmother is dressed, and you're waiting in your pyjama bottoms and T-shirt for her to name the adult relative you'll wake up to drive her to the hospital.

But she doesn't give anyone's name. "Got your Learner's Licence?" she asks you, referring to the permit your libertarian, wild-west government issued to you so you could start practising driving when you were just fourteen years old.

You're nodding. "Yeah."

She lets out a long, heavy breath. "Good enough."

You guide her into your grandfather's titanic steel car with doors that are more like airplane wings – heavy and nearly im-

possible for you to swing closed. You drive slowly and pain-
fully while you grandmother directs you through the wide,
empty streets.

"Left – left – right – that was a stop sign."

She's leading you to where the brown brick box of a hospital is lit up against the foothills of the Rocky Mountains.
You've pulled the driver's seat up as far as it will go, and you
still have to sit perched on the outermost edge of the maroon
velour so your toe can reach the pedals on the floor. Every time
you try to use the turn signal lights you end up switching on
the windshield wipers instead.

"Sorry – sorry," you keep saying – to your grandmother, to
the car, to yourself, it really doesn't matter.

The night triage nurse at the hospital glances up as you tear
a numbered ticket from the fire-alarm-red dispenser bolted to
the wall of the nearly empty emergency room. The nurse has
already looked back down at her paperwork by the time she
begins to speak.

"Over here, dear."

"I've come with my grandmother," you begin with even
more than the usual meekness you had back in those days. "She
fell – off the – the –"

"How old?" The nurse looks up over the counter.

"I'm fifteen. But I have my Learner's Licence so – "

"No. Not you, dear. How old is your grandmother?"

"Oh. Uh, seventy-something – I'm pretty sure," you stammer. "She fell and hurt her arm. Badly, I think."

"Have you got her health care card?"

"Oh, sure." You fumble through the bulky wallet you've

taken from your grandmother's purse until you find a green and white, dog-eared scrap of paper.

The nurse takes it and lifts her eyebrows, raising rows of parallel wrinkles across her forehead. "Okay. Something's not right here. It says your grandmother's first name is 'Elijah?'"

You've accidentally given the nurse your grandfather's old health care card and, for some reason, the mistake seems grave enough to make you gasp and snatch it out of her hand. You do a lot of sighing as you look for the right one, further back in the wallet, behind a stack of senior's discount cards.

The nurse jabs at her keyboard, probably unaware she's frowning again. She looks like she's about the same age as your mother so you're trying to get yourself to think of her as someone benevolent.

Her chair squeals as she rises and leaves the high-walled, melamine fortress of the admissions desk. She takes hold of one of the wheelchairs folded up and lined along the wall behind her. With a quick jerk of her thick, bare arms she throws the chair open and kicks it locked with the soft sole of her shoe.

"Alrighty," she addresses your grandmother, much too loudly even for her hearing. "Into the chair and we'll take you right over to X-ray."

The nurse turns her head toward you as she wheels your grandmother away. "You wait here," she calls. The wheelchair moves smoothly on its axles and hardly slows at all as a pair of doors with word "Restricted" stencilled across it in red letters parts in front of it.

There's a row of chairs lined up against a pink wall beside a rack of tattered magazines. You sit down in the chairs and read the scandal headlines off the magazine covers, but you don't actually touch any of them. Your mother always says reading the magazine in a medical waiting room is just like licking the spout of a public water fountain. In a moment, all you have left to read are the words on the seniors' discount cards in your grandmother's wallet. You raise them to your face and sniff. They smell like copper and leather and that stiff white lotion she calls cold cream.

And that's where you sit while the cranky babies cough against their croup and the drunks vomit onto the hard, white floor. Wind blasts into the hospital with every backward slide of the motion-sensing doors to the outside. It's nearly dawn and the hospital is starting to fill up with people who haven't slept all night. The wind they let inside helps to refresh the waiting room air a little, but you still raise the wallet to your face like a nosegay over and over again.

The restricted doors at the back of the waiting area spring open and a man dressed in a wrinkled green uniform with tufts of black hair showing through the V of fabric at the base of his throat comes walking out. His head is down, and he's walking right into the centre of the waiting room. You'd think he was a janitor if it weren't for the stethoscope draped around his neck like a spoiled cat. He announces your surname into the waiting room.

You're on your feet. "I'm her granddaughter."

"Here all by yourself?"

You look over each of your shoulders. "Yes."

He almost shrugs as he looks down at the notes scrawled on the chart in his hands. "So Grandma broke her arm, all right. That's not a surprise, really. She's about the right age to be having breakages." He still isn't looking at you – still doesn't see your age or your fear. Maybe it's deliberate. It doesn't really matter. Now he's pointing to his own flesh to help describe how and where the ends of the broken bone lie unmoored inside your grandmother's arm. You wince and squirm, and he still doesn't see.

"So we've set the bone and casted up the arm," the doctor goes on, "but we haven't released her yet because she's…" He stops and coughs – almost nervously like an ordinary human being. "Well, Grandma's a little overwrought. Crying a lot. Can't seem to get a hold of herself."

That's all he needs to say to raise your anxiety to a level just below the threshold of panic. But he keeps talking.

"It may have to do with the shot we gave her – just a little something for the pain, nothing out of the ordinary. But there's a very small portion of people who don't handle that kind of drug very well – almost like an allergy." He flicks his eyes down toward your face and you suspect he might still have grandparents of his own – distant and austere, and every bit as incapable of sleep or tears as your own. "I just thought you should know what to expect before we bring you back to see her," he finishes.

"See her," you repeat, ragged and slow. Then you know. The hospital people are about to take you through the restricted doors. They will present you to the distraught old stranger so you can comfort and calm her. The thing is not possible. The secret, private rescue your grandmother wanted from you is over. It's failed. You know you can't go any further on your own.

"I really – I should – " you begin. "I need to make a phone call."

Forgetful of the rule about the phone at the nursing station not being available for patient use, the hairy young doctor leads you back to the triage counter and hands you its telephone.

The phone rings and rings in the blue dawn of your grandmother's house. It's your brother Derek who finally answers.

"What are you doing on the phone? Where the heck are you?"

"I'm at the hospital – with Grammie. She fell and broke her arm. Go out to the camper and tell Dad."

"Okay."

"No, Derek. Go tell him right now."

"Okay."

"And Uncle Ned. You have to tell him too."

"Fine."

"Don't just go back to sleep – please."

"I said, okay."

The nurse is back, standing with one hand on the restricted doors. She sweeps her other hand toward you like she's Virgil trying to get started on your tour of the Underworld, or something. "Come on, now. Grandma's not herself and needs a familiar face to cheer her up. I'll take you back."

You breathe in a chestful of hospital air. They keep saying your grandmother isn't herself. It's not true. She is finally herself – right out in the open where even her granddaughter will see it and know what it means.

You follow Nurse Virgil through the restricted doors to where three gurneys sit lined along a wall, separated from each other by long yellow curtains blowing open at their edges with the currents of the air conditioner. A curtain edge parts slightly as you come near, and you glimpse a boy who looks a little older than you, just about dead drunk, lying on his side with a blue kidney pan pushed against his face. Another nurse jabs at the top of his hand with an IV needle. He sings a moan into the pink sheets.

Nurse Virgil pulls back the curtain by the bed farthest from the entrance and holds it open while you step through the breach. On a narrow bed, a small, shaking figure lies tucked under a thermal blanket – the kind that's kept in a warming closet for people in shock.

"We've got your granddaughter here," the nurse calls to the heap on the bed.

It sputters and shakes.

"Have a seat there, dear," the nurse says without looking at either of you.

The curtain rattles to a close on its plastic hooks, and she is gone. You are left alone with your grandmother. "Looks like they've got you all fixed up, eh Grammie?" you chirp in a clinically light voice. "We can head home as soon as you're feeling a little better."

Something turns under the blanket. There is nothing like recognition in the face looking out at you. The long pretense of intimacy between you and your grandmother crumbles. You are strangers now, as you have always been. She moves her hands to cover her face and seems startled at the stiff, white bandages swathed around her arm.

She begins speaking into her fingertips. "I will send you Elijah the prophet," she quotes, "before the coming of the great and dreadful day–"

"It's okay, Grammie," you croak, interrupting the Bible verse she's reciting – the one from the very end of the Old Testament. "It's okay. You fell on your arm in the basement. Remember? The saw bench? But – but it's alright now. We're at the hospital, and you're okay – mostly okay."

It's a credit to your under-developed sense of compassion that you know to lean forward, taking hold of the small hand your grandmother uses to cover her face. Its fingers spring closed on your own hand, trap-like, pulling you into the hollow of her throat, between the tendons of her neck.

"I will send you Elijah," she repeats, loudly and clearly between the drawn curtains, "lest I come and smite the earth with a curse."

You're glancing over both your shoulders again, but there's still no interpreter, no adaptor, no one else but you.

Your grandmother's eyes drift off to the right, and she speaks so softly you can't hear her. In a moment, her shaking subsides until it's almost stilled. She grows so quiet you're afraid. You're pulling your hand away – leaving to find Virgil, to get help – but her fingers are suddenly strong against your skin, pressing white, oval impressions of her fingertips into your flesh. You can't go anywhere.

And the poisoned boy is shedding green film from his stomach again, two curtains away.

Time passes in the emergency ward – in this tiny curtained block of space big enough for just the two of you and the clock spinning its hands over your grandmother's bed. Outside, there's a shuffling of feet and the hospital curtain clicks open behind you. Nurse Virgil flings it back far enough to make way for the substantial forms of both your parents. The small gurney is exposed to the rest of ward. The curtain won't close around all five of you, so Virgil leaves it hanging open.

"Well, will you take a look at this rescue party?" your Dad says. "It's our girl."

At the sound of her son's voice, your grandmother opens her eyes, skittish and alarmed.

"Took a fall tonight, did you, Mom?" your mother says, moving forward to smooth the blanket over the end of the thin mattress.

Your grandmother pushes your hand back at you. Her eyes trace the length of your arm to the shoulder, up your neck, and into your face. And all at once, the creases etched into the woman's face seem to twist and crack. And you know you have betrayed her.

# Six

Sometimes, usually when the weather is bad and the freeways are black with ice and the commute takes too long, you try it on – my death. You take it in – shallow but still very much beneath your skin. It's a tiny injection of grief and fear. It's meant to protect us, like an inoculation. You stand in our kitchen as the sky outside gets darker, and you let this contrived, imaginary tragedy immunize you against real sorrow. In your imagination, you marshal the possibility of my death into the small, controlled sphere – one you hope cannot coexist in the same world as a truly dead me. It's a bit like Halloween – playing dead, acting it out to keep real death away.

I'm late again tonight. You turn the lights on, pull the food out of the refrigerator, get the older boys to set the table, glance out at the weather, check the phones again, and wait.

When I finally come walking into the kitchen from the garage in my shiny black shoes, you look up at me from your cooking and our kids.

"Oh, there he is," you begin, talking over the heads of the little boys who're chattering and hugging me by my knees and waist. You're nothing like gushing with relief at seeing me, but you're not quite acting normally either.

"Look boys, Daddy's come back to us. And here I've already gone to the trouble of picking out hymns to sing at your funeral, Brigs. Hey, do you think bringing a string quartet into the chapel would be over the top? I mean, as long as you're dead I should be able to afford it, what with all that life insurance blood money and everything."

I drop my keys on the counter. "I'm sorry. I didn't mean to be late. Someone came into my office to talk to me right at five o'clock, and I couldn't get away."

"And so you turned off your phone, naturally."

You're standing over the countertop where a small, dead, raw chicken is dripping a thick, pink fluid onto a block of wood. There's a knife in your hand – one of those astoundingly expensive ones people only buy from salesmen-relatives who are down on their luck. You're using it to carve a leg off the chicken carcass. Everything you do in the kitchen looks so easy – the way you separate an egg or roll a meatball onto its raw side without having it crumble into bits in the frying pan. Even this precise mutilation of the chicken – where you take the animal apart as if it was never held together with anything more than tiny, invisible zippers – there's a kind of perfection to it. It's gorgeous. And it'd make you even madder than you already are if I mention it.

But that's not what I'm thinking as I pull my cell phone out of my pocket to prove you're wrong about me shutting it off. "See, I didn't – what? I did not turn it – ah, dang it. I must have forgotten to switch the ringer back on after my morning meeting. Sorry.

But having your cell phone ring in the middle of a meeting like that is the worst. It's like openly passing gas or something."

"Anyways," you go on, flipping the chicken over to cut off its wings. "I thought each of your sisters could offer prayers at your memorial service. But I couldn't decide which one of your cousins I should ask to give the eulogy. I mean, ideally I'd do it myself, but since speaking at your mother's funeral was almost emotionally impossible for me, I decided I'd better assign it to someone else, right? Someone who's kind of close but kind of far away at the same time."

That's when I cross the floor to hug you into the crackling down fill and nylon of my winter coat. You've still got the knife in your hand but I'll hold onto you anyway – at least until I feel you starting to straighten and strain away from me.

"Brigs – Brigs, my hands are covered in chicken gunk."

When you say it, I can smell it. I let go and you step away to take hold of what's left of the chicken. There's a crack as its vertebrae come apart in your bare hands.

"By the way," you go on, "you still haven't given me definitive permission to have all your loveliness cremated. I need something in writing in case anyone tries to get up in my face with their nonsense about 'desecration.'"

To the snap and sting of static electricity, I slide my heavy coat off my arms. I'm kicking through the pile of winter boots and coats and mittens strewn in front of the hall closet. The floor is wet with melted snow, soaking through my socks. It looks like the boys came home from school and then just exploded inside the front door.

"Okay, okay. Enough with the funeral planning," I say. "I

made it home just fine."

"And for floral tributes," you continue as you break through the marrow of the chicken's sternum with the knife blade, "I guess we'll go with whatever's in season – and not too girlie. Only no lilies. Lilies have a terrible smell. There, I said it."

I sniff. "You don't like lilies?"

"Hate 'em."

I cock my head. "I must not remember what they smell like."

"Well, it's one of those pricky smells that gets right up inside your cribriform plate."

I snort. "All right. No funeral lilies. How about some fancy orchids then – something to go with the string quartet?"

"Yuck, no."

"Come on. You can't hate all the over-priced flowers on principle."

"It's got nothing to do with principles. It's just that orchids–" You pause to roll your eyes at yourself over the dismembered chicken. "I wouldn't have to explain this to you if you hadn't been too busy with all that math to ever take a zoology class in university."

"Huh?"

"You've never dissected a rat, Brigs."

I'm shaking my head as you step away from the tray of neatly arranged, butchered chicken pieces to wash your hands in the sink. "Are we still picking out my funeral flowers?" I ask.

"Yes. I'm sorry. But the fact is the look of certain kinds of orchids reminds me of – rat testes."

I laugh so loudly the boys join in from the living room, even though they don't know why they're doing it. You lunge at me — clean, wet hands on my dress shirt — and push against my chest with both your palms.

"It's not funny. And it's not something I like about myself."

I don't try very hard to straighten my face. "No, of course it's not."

"Then stop laughing about it. It's awful. My zoology lab partner was some kind of crazy person, and she came back from the bin full of dead rats with the frickin' Alpha Male for us to dissect. He was so virile the lab instructor called the whole class over to marvel at his gonads after we finished skinning them. And then she made me stand there and point at every bit of his reproductive anatomy with a probe while I told everyone what everything was called and what he used to do with it. It was a nightmare. And they — the things — they looked almost exactly like pink lady slipper orchids."

I'm still laughing a little but I'm trying to apologize for it at the same time.

You give me one more shove and I finally see the red glassiness in your eyes — like you're not that far from starting to cry. "Orchids look exactly like rat testes," you say. "And after the dissection, the smell of the rat stayed with me for the rest of the day. It was in my hair, or in my brain, like another one of my stupid post-traumatic stress reactions. Stop — it's not funny. I've never been the same since."

You let me hug you for a moment. When you lean away from me, you brace my head between your hands and pull my forehead down to yours. "So no orchids at our funerals, okay?"

"Right. Absolutely no orchids under any circumstances."

You're stepping away from me, eager to move on.

I'm nodding, grinning. "So," I say, catching your hand, kneading your palm with my thumb, "you didn't get around to planning a second marriage for yourself, did you?"

"Gross, Brigs. I'm standing here, staging my mourning for you, and you're asking me - "

"Sorry. Sorry." And I'm gathering you into me again, against my shoulder in that way I know I can't hold for very long before your hyper-flexed neck starts to hurt. "Anyway, I made it home just fine."

"I know you made it this time. But it's scary when – I shouldn't even be here, I shouldn't even know you."

"Don't start with that again–-"

You're holding my hand again, running the edge of one fingernail along the length of the bone below my forefinger. The pressure leaves a white line in my skin that disappears moments later. You're speaking again. "Here you are married to me when I'm not even good enough to have coffee with you."

"We don't drink coffee."

"Everyone knows I shouldn't be here. The waitress in the restaurant last weekend who asked if we wanted separate cheques because, clearly, there's no way you would actually be with me – even that girl knew it. Everyone knows it but you."

None of this is anything I haven't heard you say over and over again. It always leaves me feeling strange – flattered and guilty, awed by the ridiculous proportions of your feelings but sad, like it might be my fault.

And that's when I bend my face all the way down to yours, low enough to kiss you. "Hey now," I say as I pull away, "there's nothing that can take me away from here."

You aren't looking at me. All I can see when I try to find your face is your hair. It's long and loose and I can barely discern half a dozen tiny keratin crescent moons – little slivers of our boys' freshly cut fingernails – tangled where they flew off the end of a pair of clippers and into the net of your hair. I raise my hand and start to work at removing them from the strands.

You swallow. "There is something that can take you away. There's what almost happened tonight. There's death."

I scoff. "Come on. We're great with death. Death is our thing. Ask anyone in the family."

"That's it exactly," you say, quietly. "It's like death has been specially grooming us for something for years."

"Nah. Death is grooming everybody. It's just that not everyone knows not to slink off somewhere and hate it."

You're just shaking your head, moving back to the counter, spooning the runny red sauce you've made over the skin of the chicken pieces. You won't say anything more – as if you're afraid to make any kind of answer out loud. ·

And that's the end of it, even though the question of my funeral flowers is still far from settled, and I haven't told you which of my cousins to ask to speak for me when I'm gone. I haven't even given you the permission you wanted to cremate my body. But the boys are cantering around the kitchen telling you how good everything smells and how hungry they are. So this will be the end of it until the next time, when you manage to keep me alive a little longer, moving through this pantomime of my death, here in the house, after dark, without me.

# Seven

Remembering the clatter and slam of the front screen door, you come back into your grandmother's house on the morning of your grandfather's funeral through the back entrance. Inside, you find your Uncle Ned, fully dressed except for his socks, leaning forward in a chair with his forehead pressed against the hard surface of the kitchen tabletop. He sits up at the clicking of the door clasp.

"You're back," he says, rubbing at the red line in his forehead where he knows the edge of the table has left its imprint.

"Mom just dropped me off," you say. "She's gone back to the hospital already."

"Yeah, you got me in trouble with your Mom. Thanks a lot, kiddo. I wish you'd come to me for help last night." Uncle Ned is smirking as he rises to his feet. He pours a glass of orange juice as he stands in front of the open door of the refrigerator. Even you know it's not one of those new, frost-free fridges, and he should shut the door before the glacier in the freezer compartment inches down any further.

"Sorry. Grammie never asked me to go get anyone else to help."

Uncle Ned snorts. "No. No, I don't suppose she would have. So how is she doing, anyways?"

"Oh – um," you stammer, your neck flushing red. "She'll be okay. But her arm's in a cast all the way to the elbow." Your hand clasps your own elbow and you pause long enough to make Uncle Ned look up from his juice. He's still standing in the open refrigerator. "And – um – she did have a bit of a bad reaction to the – medication – they gave her for the pain."

He chuckles and closes the refrigerator door. "A bad trip, eh? I suppose we should have seen that coming. Mom's definitely not what anyone would call 'mellow.'"

You watch Uncle Ned standing on the linoleum in his bare feet. He's leaning on the edge of the kitchen sink. "I'd better get over to the hospital, I guess," he says, tipping the remaining inch of his juice down the drain.

He leaves, the unfastened metal buckles of his sandals jingling away across the dewless back lawn. The gate closes with a dry clatter of wooden planks, and then his luxury pickup truck roars out of sight down the alleyway. As the engine noise fades, you hear something else in the old house – another voice, a woman. You crane your neck around the corner of the kitchen wall until you can see her, standing at the screen door at the front of the house.

A woman you've never seen before stands outside the screen. She's dressed in office clothes – high-heeled shoes and a cream-coloured suit that's badly creased across her hips. Her bone-thin hand holds a large floral wreath. Her face is cast in one of those automatic, professional office smiles as she talks through the wire mesh to Uncle Ned's daughter, your cousin Janae.

"So maybe I'm at the wrong house," you hear the woman say through the screen. "I'm looking for – Ned?"

Janae doesn't say a word. You start to wonder if she's really awake – if she's sleepwalking, or something. But her stance in the doorway isn't loose and sleepy. It's taut and alert – almost convulsing.

The woman just keeps talking. "I'm a co-worker of Ned's. From his firm in Calgary."

Janae makes no move to open the door. "I know who you are," she says. Her voice scares you. It's not the voice of fourteen-year-old Janae, but her elemental voice – ageless.

Outside, the woman's face turns ashy around her lipstick and she coughs against the back of her free hand. "We all wanted to send some flowers with our respects but we weren't sure which funeral home the family's using. The obituary must not have run in the Calgary papers – "

"No. Why would it?" Janae answers in the same voice as before. It's too much. You're stepping out of the kitchen – past your sleeping brothers in the living room – moving to jostle Janae out of whatever's got a hold of her.

As you advance, the woman extends the flowers toward the closed screen door – gladiolas, white carnations, and large, rigid lilies pocked at the bases of their petals with little bumps, like skin tags. The smell of the lilies stings at your nose with a scent like the pearly white antiseptic soap dripping from dispensers hung in the hospital bathrooms. You can tell from Janae's posture that her arms are folded over her flat middle. She will not open the door to receive the flowers. The woman can see that and stoops to lay the wreath on the concrete step outside.

"Please give Ned our best wishes," she says, almost meekly, and she turns away, moving down the walkway.

You're not sure if Janae knows you're there, standing behind her, listening along with her to the soles of the high-heeled shoes scraping grit into the face of the concrete. Janae's head droops toward her chest, bringing the white wreath into her view. Its pricking sweetness seeps into the house like chemical warfare, borne on the small wind moving through the mesh of the metal screen.

A rush of air breaks on your face as the screen door rattles open under Janae's hands. She's got the wreath in her fingers and her bare feet are slapping up the walkway. Her hands claw the flowers free and hurl them away from the house in handfuls, her fingers stained yellow with all the pollen. She wants to be vicious but the petals just sail delicately through the air, landing on the street and the roof of the woman's car without a sound. Mouth gaping, the woman leans back – watching as Janae chases after her – stupefied in mid-motion with just one foot planted on the floor inside her car.

You can hear the gasping – the noise Janae makes as she fights for air, struggling like she's dreaming through a bout of sleep apnea – like she's you, grown up and dreaming of the bodies of the Incorrupt Saints. You step through the screen door and run to her. And as you touch her shoulder, her throat opens.

"Don't–you–come–here!" she chokes at the woman, hurling fern fronds and white petals onto the dusty hood of the car. "Don't–you–dare–come–here!"

The woman stands frozen for an instant longer, watching speechless as the girl finishes tearing the flowers and greenery out of the wreath and starts pulling apart the arrangement's foam core. It dissolves easily under the pressure of Janae's fingers. A chip of foam lands with a dull ring on the hood of the car. The sound seems to jar the stranger out of her stupor and frees her to duck inside the vehicle, closing and locking the doors. She drives away, watching both of you in her rear-view mirror as she goes. A cloud of shattered flowers blows off her car and on to the pavement, strewn all over the road like the battered, browning, trailing petals of a wedding procession.

It isn't much later in the same day when you stand in front of the enormous mirror bolted to the dark wooden dresser in your grandmother's spare bedroom. Janae is standing beside you, dressed for the chapel, curling her glossy brown hair with a hot metal barrel. Even though you're on your feet, you're stunned and exhausted past the point of sleepiness. You're connected to wakefulness by the smell in the room – deep and organic – of the human oils and proteins superheated and denatured along the shafts of Janae's limp funeral ringlets.

You hold the palm of your right hand up to the mirror and look at its lines reflected in the glass. You're halfway through your teen years, and you've never had your future read from your palm – not counting the time you borrowed that book on palmistry from the town library. Remember that book – the one with the blue satin binding and the crusty smear of yellowed glue where a plastic gem used to be attached to the cover? I think they had a copy of the same book in the young adult section of the library in my town – complete with nothing but dried glue left where the jewel should have been. Of

69

course, neither of us believes in any of that goofy occult stuff. But we each independently read *The Young Diviner's Guide to Palmistry* anyway. At the time, it just felt like something we should know.

You've forgotten which one of the cracks in your palm is called a life line. It must be the long one, you hope, as you trace your finger along its curve around the mound at the base of your thumb. Another one of the deepest lines, you remember, is supposed to be for love. That's me – there in the mirror with you, even then. But you don't know anything about me yet so you just close your hand.

At fifteen, your skin runs smooth and tight over your skull without any lines at all. Before last night in the hospital with Grammie, your unlined face would have been perfectly matched to the fact that nothing much has ever really happened to you. How come we never hear about fortune tellers who read the lines in faces instead of hands? Maybe it's because we're born with lines in our palms but the lines in our faces only come with time. Faces must only be good for reading the past.

Beside you in the mirror, Janae has heard all she can stand of nothing but the clicking of her curling iron. You've waited all day, but she hasn't said anything about the lady at the door this morning. It's getting harder and harder to remember that crisis at all. It's being eclipsed by the day's next crisis – the crisis of your grandfather's dead body. You will be faced with it in a little over an hour at a service the adults in the family are calling "the viewing."

Janae has her mind ground into the same morbid rut. "It won't look hardly anything like him," she says, all at once. She knows because she went to a funeral on her mother's side of the family when she was eleven years old. "You'll think you're at the wrong person's funeral when you first see it."

"Maybe we shouldn't be calling Granddad's body an 'it,'" you suggest, even though the two of you have tacitly agreed Janae is the expert on funerals — the Niagara Falls mummies notwithstanding, I guess.

She shrugs into the mirror. Her parents' separation, her great-aunt's funeral, attacking her father's mistress with flower petals, a handful of other disappointments you couldn't possibly know about — they've all hardened her. She's all bravado and bad manners. She's arguing. "Why not call an 'it' an 'it?' I mean, it's not like Granddad's body is all that human anymore — no spirit, no blood, weird make-up all over him. Why do they drain all the blood out of dead bodies anyway? Like, what's the harm in keeping it? And what do they even do with it all once it's out? Just wash it down the sink into the water supply, or whatever? As if that's sanitary."

An hour later, sleepless and sad, you stand beside the open coffin, exhaling in deep, slow breaths, looking over the waxy yellowness they say is the body of your first grandfather to die. Maybe Janae was right. The pronoun "it" doesn't quite describe what you see — but neither does "him." Despite the empty, pinched look of the nose, you decide death's harshest marks fall on the hands. The embalmers have heaped them together over the body's middle, where they rest against the white fabric of the grave clothes. The skin hangs downward from the hands like loose, leather mitts. But maybe, in his seventies, Granddad's hands already looked like that before he died. You can't remember.

And you can't see the lower half of the body at all. The coffin lid is split in two, and the lower portion is already closed and covered with a pile of white roses and carnations. You heard your mother call the flowers a "spray" as if it was flung up out of the ocean, from a thousand miles away, all by itself. Actually, you're not wondering how the flowers got there at all. You don't know yet – not like we do now – that nothing at a funeral appears all on its own. Someone has to sit down and make up his mind and draw it out of somewhere – choice after choice after bloody choice.

When the time allotted for everyone to "view" the body is over, the funeral director steps forward to close the lid of the coffin.

"Excuse me," he says as he reaches past you. But then, even though you're a kid, he remembers himself and straightens up. "I'm sorry. Are you finished?"

You nod, and he presses the lid into place. Maybe he's specially trained to close it without a sound. Or maybe it's one of those options the bereaved get to choose while they're sitting in the family consultation room with their chequebooks open. "Mark this box for audible casket closure."

After the lid is shut, and the sight of the body is hidden, the whispers in the room grow a little louder. In a moment, there will be a prayer, and then you'll all follow the coffin on its bier down the long church hallway to the vaulted chapel for the memorial service.

You glance behind yourself to where your family sits. Your grandmother is there, of course, perched in a chair with her ankles crossed, her feet not quite touching the blue carpet on the floor, her arm in its cast laid across her lap. You still haven't spoken to her since you left her at the hospital.

Her older grandsons – your brothers and cousins – will be among the pall bearers today. Little red rose appliqués are pinned to the lapels of their cheap starter suits so the funeral directors will be able to keep track of them all. One of your brothers slipped past your parents wearing a novelty necktie printed to look like it's made from yellow police tape strung around a crime scene. There's nothing anyone can do about it now.

The grandsons' full names are written in columns inside the keepsake funeral program. Someone said there's a black limousine waiting in the church parking lot to ferry them all to the cemetery just outside the town – the cemetery sitting on the side of a hill in view of a custom cattle feed lot. The grandsons are funerary rock stars – the pall-boys standing in a misshapen circle, their long bangs hanging over their eyes, their bony shoulders slouching away from the stiff, moulded forms of their suits.

No one seems to be looking at you – a small, teen-aged girl – standing pressed to the side of the closed coffin. Behind the screen of your body, you slide your hand along the brass bar bolted to the shiny wood. The metal is cold, and your fingers leave steamy clouds wherever you've touched it.

And you know you're not really the person you want to be yet. If you were, you would be beckoning Janae to come join you.

"I need to hold him," your best self would have told your cousin. "Help me. We need to hold him for ourselves, or we might not feel good ever again."

And both of you would have closed your hands around the yellow metal. The muscles inside your arms would have hardened as the mass of both your bodies shifted away from the coffin. You would have tipped and flexed until, very slightly, one edge of the coffin was lifted up, out of the chrome-plated bier, borne by your strength. And then your arms would loosen again, bending into soft, white curves, the raised edge of the coffin coming back to rest – back to where the pall-boys would be able to find it when the time came to take it all away.

Your Mom's hand is on you now. "Come sit down, honey. What a day you've had."

You let go of the metal bar, walking sideways under your mother's arm, watching the clouds left from the moisture of your hands fading to vapour on the brass. And then your feet seem to lock and you won't be moved another step.

"No," you say.

Your Mom is frowning. Both of her arms are around you now. The strength is still there – your mother's irresistible power summoned here from faraway in your early childhood. She's talking right into your ear, low and unequivocal. "Come on, now. Not today."

And you're moving again, away from the coffin, back to the crowd waiting on padded folding chairs. How can they not know it when they look at you? All of this – the basement, the hospital curtains, the mirror, whatever's left of Elijah – maybe a part of this does belong to the pall-boys and your bossy cousin and your angry uncles and your broken grandmother. Yet somehow, at last, you know it's rightfully yours.

# Eight

People – like my mother – are able to fall down and just die of heart attacks or dengue fever or kidney failure or any of the other millions of natural causes of human mortality. But the paperwork people leave behind is different. Nature has no interest in it at all. Instead, someone needs to round it all up, stand it in a line, and manually kill off the paperwork, one shred at a time.

Through some unspoken kind of collective consciousness, everyone in my family agreed that Mom would have wanted me – the oldest of her kids, the one who was already waist deep in her death – to be the one to finish winding up her estate. I think they may have thought it was my birthright as her first-born or something stupid like that. It might be true that some people consider appointing a person as their executor to be an honour. Only, it's not an honour. It's one final, parting kick in the shins.

At least Mom's estate is simple and impoverished with no real property left in it. For a few thousand dollars, she'd turned over her portion of the house where I was raised to my Dad when she left him. He'd turned around and sold it as soon as my little brother wandered away from home for good. The people who own the house now keep a flock of chickens in the yard and park their cars all over the grass. It's not right.

Anyway, with no house, and with the police having already impounded her car for all those traffic tickets she never had any hope of paying, my lawyer friend assured me we could probably handle her estate business without ever needing to go to court. He rapid-fired a pep talk on our jurisdiction's estate laws at me, let me make a sheet of written notes from our conversation, and made me promise never to mention his name. And then, by degrees, unintentionally, I ended up letting you take over the whole mess yourself.

Mom's estate is completely your project by the time I stand behind you as you click away on our big desktop computer. Sloppy stacks of old receipts line both of your thighs as you sit cross-legged on a folding metal chair with your feet tucked under your knees. You hand me one of the stacks of receipts without taking your eyes off the screen.

"Shred these, if you please," you instruct me.

The little squares of paper are mostly from the gas station convenience store in Mom's small town.

"You wouldn't think a diabetic would buy that much cola, would you?" you say when you sense that I've started squinting behind you, trying to read the fading print on the receipts.

"Sugar-free cola, right?" I ask.

"Nope."

I smirk. There's nothing we can do to save her now. "Well, I'm sure Mom chased her sugar cola with big shots of insulin so all the math worked out when it was time to answer to her blood tests."

No one knows how to cope with a big problem – diabetes, obesity, a rotten marriage, rotten kids – better than people who don't have to live with it themselves.

You hum back at the buzzing glass tube in front of you. "Yeah, it's too bad diabetes isn't really the numbers game some people like to think it is. Isn't that right, Benny?" you ask the baby I'm holding.

In the crook of my arm, I hold our littlest son turned outward so he can merrily kick and punch – baby-sparring with the open air as he watches you work. The whir and tear of the paper shredder charges his muscles with something and makes his movements even more animated.

As far as babies go, big Benny is fantastic. He's always been huge for his age – so big there was a sound from your skin like a leather couch getting ripped open at the moment he was born. The nurse actually looked up at me and said, "Did you *hear* that?"

All the typical terror and pain was supposed to be over by the time Benny's birth really started to scare me. It happened as the doctor was putting you back together and you lost your grip on – everything.

Your head fell back against the bed. "Goin' out," was all you said.

They brought you back with a shot of blood coagulant and an oxygen mask.

Here at home, baby Benny needs to be fed an awful lot, and he still wakes you up in the night, but we both adore him anyway.

Jennifer Quist

Maybe it's not so much that Benny's fantastic. Maybe it's just that, now that we're raising a baby for the fourth time, we've finally learned not to be mad at him for all the things he can't deliver.

Benny is the baby who was with us – invisible, not quite created – the day we found Mom's body, almost a year ago. So I guess it's only fitting that he's here with us now, at the end of her story. At the funeral, Benny was a secret between just you and me. And we kept him a secret until you were almost six months into his gestation, like a couple of teenagers who couldn't deal with their unplanned pregnancy. It didn't matter how long or legal or stable our marriage was when I knocked you up with Benny. It was still a catastrophe.

That was last spring. Now, with Benny all perfect and whole in my arms, I look down to where the white plane of the computer screen in front of the three of us is split into a grid. You tell me it's a spreadsheet proving that my mother died completely bankrupt.

We'll make a dozen copies of it and mail it away, enclosed with terse letters explaining that no one is getting any of the money they're owed out of Mom's estate – nothing, never. There's no money for the ex-husbands, the credit card companies, the dentist she'd been threatening to sue, or even the federal tax office itself.

The pile of bills she left behind contains demand letters addressed to every different name she used – our name, her father's name, the names of each one of her husbands including the ones she didn't even like.

Her veterinarian landlord never wants to see us again, so he took his damage deposit a long time ago and accepted it was all he'd ever get to cover her back rent – not to mention the total annihilation of the Dead Lady Trailer.

The credit card companies came at us with false sympathy, offering to clear her debts if we'd agree to pay half of the amounts she owed. We were legally entitled to refuse to pay for anything, so we did. The most obnoxious creditor of all was the long-distance phone company bent against all decency on getting their final fifty-eight dollar bill paid. One of the call centre supervisors was on the other end of the line the day you finally cracked.

"She's dead, okay? Dead – D-E-A-D – otherwise known to you people as 'the cost of doing business.'"

A stack of plain security-lined envelopes are already stamped and marked with just Mom's now-defunct post office box number as a return address. If anyone wants to find us to threaten or sue us, they'll have to work for it. They'll have to work their way past you – standing here in front of me, white and shining in the glare of the computer screen.

# Nine

We've met him just once since he turned thirtyish and paunchy and his forehead spread all the way back to his mid-head. It was at the wedding reception of one of the hundreds of distant relatives I share with him – all of us the descendants of one of the original Abrahams of the dry farmlands barely north of the American border. I'm grinning and smug under all my perfectly preserved brown hair as we walk away from him.

You poke me with your elbow and tell me again how when he was yours, when you were both sixteen years old, he was beautiful – a lithe and gloomy Peter Pan, his dark bangs hanging all the way down over one eye, his thin shoulders draped in a long black coat bought from the only army surplus store for hundreds of kilometres. But I know you've got a generous and tolerant sense of physical beauty, so I'm still not convinced.

There's no need to argue it with you because you're already laughing, moving past it like it's all completely embarrassing. I don't have to say a word to get you to admit that you still don't know what it was that used to make you want to love him so badly. Maybe it was an effect of some kind of chemical intoxicant wafting up from the wet, broken pineapple weed he pulverized against the cracked sidewalks with every turn of the wheels of his glinting grey skateboard.

"You know, he never actually called me his girlfriend, in all that time. He preferred to say we were just 'involved.' Sixteen-year-old kids – involved – isn't that hilarious, Brigs?"

Somehow, I'm not laughing. And I'm glad we're driving away from him, moving away from another one of those pink and yellow wedding receptions.

"Blush and butter-cream," you correct me.

You don't mind the spin the bride's given the colours' names, but you are complaining about having to sit through a read-ing of that sappy poem with the forced, awkward rhyme for the third time this year. Our sweet, earnest relatives can't seem to stop themselves from sniffling through it at all the family weddings now.

"'... a special dress, like very other few...'" you quote from the poem. The lines have got you shuddering behind the steer-ing wheel. "Very other few."

On the passenger side of the car I'm not really listening to this rant I've heard just as many times as I've heard the poem itself. Instead, I'm remembering the story you told me about a stupid fight you had with my distant cousin who used to kiss you right on the mouth. He picked the fight right there on the sidewalk outside your high school, in front of everyone. It started when he glided up beside you – unnaturally tall on his skateboard – with a wrinkled paper bag from the drug store crammed into his pocket. He pushed the bag into your hands – and that was when he asked you to dye his hair black.

I smirk again. "Didn't he totally lose it that time you told him his eyebrows wouldn't match his hair if he made you dye it black?"

Then you're laughing at me for still thinking about him. Maybe it is weird. It's too late to take back my prying now. You've already started re-telling the old legends about him – like it's been too long since you first told me these stories, and you're ready to repeat them.

Yes, he was mad about the hair dye. He didn't understand the caterpillar prominence of the thick, light brown brows over his eyes – knew nothing of the embarrassing drama in the way the stray hairs reached out for each other over the hard, white bridge of his nose. But he found satisfaction in anger, especially when it came to you. And it was with a tiny trace of pleasure that he nearly tore the paper bag as he snatched it out of your hands – glaring and rolling away, leaving the other kids on the lawn of the high school to gape at you.

For hours afterward, he ignored you – right up until he slid a note folded like a foolscap crane into the reveal of your locker door. I've seen the note myself, much later – flattened but still creased from his origami. I found it when we were moving house, and it fell onto the floor out of your old copy of *The Fountainhead*, as I packed up the bookcase.

"On the coulee at sunset. Me."

You explain that there was going to be a planet visible in the sky that night: Jupiter. "Or maybe it was Mars," you tell me.

He claimed that, for once, all you'd need to see way out to Jupiter was your naked eyes. Even though he said the word "naked" right to your face, you still agreed to ask your Mom if you could use the car to drive out past the light pollution of the town and into the countryside that night.

Just before dark, there you were, sitting with him in the dry, needle-tipped prairie grass, wondering if dew ever fell there in the ancient valley that rolled up and away from the scrawny river below like a weathered green blanket. You leaned back, straight-armed, resting on your palms, with the folded cuffs of your jeans crossed at your ankles. That's how you sat, lazy and not quite bored, looking for Jupiter – or Mars. Beside you in the grass, he would have been glaring out into space, hunched over his bent legs, closing his arms around his knees. A shiny chip of rock hung in the sky, almost too far away to see.

"He was so disgusted with me when I asked him to tell me again how we knew it wasn't just Venus."

And even though, from a distance, the scene on the sunset hillside could have been lifted right out of one of the novels on the small white bookcase in cousin Janae's bedroom, your first boy just gathered his army overcoat around his thin ribcage and pulled his eyebrows closer together. You watched his face – watched your own fingers passing lightly over the edge of his mouth where a faint constellation of tiny freckles faded into the pink of his lip. His fingers were closing around your hand, pulling it away from his face, dropping it into your lap.

"Keep your irony to yourself," he said.

You still hadn't quite become yourself yet, so you just pulled your knees up and bowed your head into them. But you promise me you did manage to mutter, "Where'd you read that?"

Riding on the plush seats of your mother's car, the bottom of your Doc Marten shoe pressed to the accelerator, you drove out of the dark, back toward the town. He was talking and talking by then – something about an apple rotting in the broken shell of a giant bug – until your foot pivoted sharply on its heel, coming down hard on the brake. In front of your mother's car, the headlights lit up a wreck glittering on the pavement. The front end of a car had crumpled against the stout, pressure-hardened post of a road sign. A splintered stump jutted out of the gravel on the roadside, but the rest of the sign was gone, launched into the oblivion of the broad black ditch between the highway and a hayfield.

"It used to be a sign for the Report-A-Poacher hotline," you tell me, shrugging. "I have no idea why I still know that. Memory is strange, eh Brigs?"

Broken glass and plastic and machinery spread like a burned out minefield across the asphalt. Two pairs of cloven-hoofed stick legs hung down over the windshield's empty gap. A bay-coloured body bled onto the roof of the car.

You and the boy both opened your car doors and stood behind them as if they were great, steel shields. Music was playing loudly from within the wreck. A gloomy British bass line from a song we all had on our mixed tapes in those days droned over the dark fields.

"It could be someone we know," your boy said, squinting down the white columns burning from the headlights of your Mom's car.

You squinted too. "Should we go look?"

His throat clicked but he actually said nothing.

You pushed the car door closed. "I'm going."

"Wait," he called, terrified, maybe, at the sight of your

wings beginning to unfurl. You're not in a basement this time – not hidden with your grandmother behind the curtains in the depths of a hospital. You're standing right out here on the road between miles and miles of open fields where anybody could see what you are.

The boy could hardly speak to you. "What – what are we supposed to do?"

You shrugged one shoulder. "How should I know? You used to be the Boy Scout. Go try 'n' flag down some help, or something."

You started down the road, away from him. His voice behind you was saying something you couldn't understand over the sound of the music but you didn't turn back.

The song grew louder near the wreck, where blood and hair and excrement smeared the car's glossy white paint. A deer carcass lay pinched in the crevice its impact had carved into the roof. The frame of the driver's window had flexed and squeezed its tempered glass out onto the highway where it was scattered at your feet, broken into little green jewels. It must have crunched under the soles of your shoes as you approached the car. But it's your English teacher's voice you're hearing, speaking inside your head – something about a ghost in the machine.

You took a breath as if diving under water and stooped to the window.

The driver was a stranger, but he was still just a little older than you were that night. The steering column had been thrust too far into the passenger compartment by the collision with the sign post – or maybe with the deer – and it rammed

85

against his chest. His shoulders lurched as he breathed against the crush.

"Are you okay?" you asked, even though you knew it was stupid.

"Get m'out," the driver said. Then he raised his fingers to keep you away. "No, don' touch."

"I won't," you said. "It's okay. My friend's gone for help."

"Don' go," he exhaled.

"I won't," you said again, squeezing your hands between your knees as you bent toward to the window. "I won't go." There must have been a trace of a tremor in your voice even though you would have tried to keep its tone light as plastic – the same voice you use now when you're at the boys' parent-teacher interviews.

The driver turned his eyelids to you. "Go's sake," he gasped. "Turn'ff music."

Before you could say anything more, another voice was pronouncing curses just behind your head. It wasn't your boy. It was a man, standing in the beam of the headlights of your mother's car, walking toward you in silhouette like a cheap effect in a music video. Every time you tell it, I wish he was me. But he isn't. You still don't know who he is. And neither do I.

"Hey, I got a cell phone here," the man said, waving a grey box. "I already dialled 9-1-1."

"Hey, did you hear that?" you sang to the driver. "Help's coming any minute now – an ambulance and everything."

"Hang in there, buddy," the man bawled into the car from over your shoulder. He bent to look more closely, swearing his face off in deepest sympathy.

The cassette deck had reached the end of the tape and was clicking in the dashboard as it automatically began rewinding the music. In the new quiet, the man with the phone straightened his back and craned his neck to look past the wreck, down the highway. You glanced at him long enough to notice the way his large, pale moustache hid his mouth. It made you want to drop your eyes to the broken glass gems at your feet. By then the man with the phone had leaned so close to you that you sprang back, covering the base of your throat with your hand.

"Hey, is that kid out there a friend of yours?" is all he said.

"Oh no," you answered, sputtering, sounding stupid and scared, "we weren't sure if we'd really found Jupiter or not but we gave up anyway and were driving back into town. And then we ran into this guy — well, we didn't run into him, literally, that must have been the deer. But we did stop and —"

"No, I don't mean the poor fella in there," man interrupted. He jerked his chin away from the wreck — away from you — motioning to the black length of highway beyond everything either of you could see. "I mean the tall kid in the long coat, walking right down the centre line in the dark. He's gonna get himself killed."

We know from the wedding reception that he didn't die on the highway — your first boy, the one dressed all in black, letting his feet pace down the yellow centre line. After the ambulance came and went, both you and the boy made it home in perfect safety that night. You even stayed entangled with one another for a little longer, though the end was clearly imminent.

It wasn't long after he showed you Jupiter that you found

him in a small garage that was once set on fire, but still stood – charred and sooty – at the back of his parents' yard. One side of it looked like it was cobbled together out of tiny coal tiles. He was inside the garage, in the dust and shade, pounding a small, one-handed sledge hammer against the concrete floor.

"He called the hammer a 'maul,'" you tell me.

You knew he liked it when you pretended he was a monster so you asked, "What are you doing? Is it time to move the body you hid under the slab already?"

He stood up, almost smiling, letting the shaft of the hammer slide through his fist.

"Check it out."

Something glinted in the dimness, and he flipped a flat copper oval into the palm of your hand. It was almost unrecogniz-able – all thin and oblong with the image of Queen Elizabeth II that's usually stamped on the metal beaten away. It had been, very recently, a penny.

The misshapen disc fell into the white flesh of your hand and you yelped. "It's hot."

He faked a scoff. "Of course it's hot. That's what you get with a kinetic energy transfer."

You shrugged one shoulder. "I never took physics."

He shook his head, but he closed an arm around your waist, pulling you against him, pressing the hammer still throttled in his hand into the small of your back, speaking down into your face. "Well, it means that the motion of the hammer transforms into heat energy when the floor forces it to stop moving. And that makes the copper not only smashed flat, but hot."

You swayed in his hold. "Seriously? That is amazing."

"Not really," he murmured, bending his face toward your neck. "You know, up close like this, you're not all that smart – "

"Nice." You jerked away.

" – and nobody knows it but me."

You twisted, bending as his mouth moved closer to your neck. He pushed your hair aside with his nose and chin. You felt his breath on your skin and couldn't help but utter a little scream as you made a pretense of dodging. You were still cackling and struggling with him when you saw a new shadow on the cement floor. Someone else was standing in the open garage doorway. He let go of you so quickly you nearly fell to the ground.

The long shadow belonged to a little girl – his youngest sister, a three-year-old in a frilly, homemade dress that made her look like a mangled wedding cake. "Dad made me stop playing and said you guys have to take care of me now," she told him.

The boy hummed. "It's the old baby-chaperone trick, is it? Well played, Dad."

You smoothed your hair with your hands. "Don't tell me your parents think I'm your girlfriend or something like that."

He pulled another round, perfect penny out of his pocket. "Kinetic energy transfer – you want to try it?"

"I try it," said the little wedding cake.

"Just stay back, okay?" he told her as he laid out the penny on the concrete.

"Well?" you persisted. "What do your parents know about me?"

He was the one shrugging now. "I don't know. We haven't talked about it. Does it matter?"

"Probably."

But he was clever too. "So what do your parents know about me?" he countered.

You flinched, walking backwards, starting to move out of the shadow of the burnt-up garage. "Look, we both know this whole thing is stupid," you said. "That's why neither of us ever talks to anyone about it."

"Wait," he said, folding your fingers down over the copper that had cooled but was still cupped in your palm. "Keep the penny."

"It is no longer a penny. Look what you did."

And you know this has to be the last time you'll turn and leave him standing there, with the hammer and the pennies and – everything.

# Ten

I'll admit it freaks me out a bit when I pick up the phone and hear a voice almost exactly like my dead mother's talking out of it. "Hi. Brigham?"

"Yes, that's me."

"Hi. It's your aunt – Aunt Deb."

Of course, the voice really belongs to my mother's younger sister. She's still alive, but I don't think I've seen her since Mom's funeral.

"Oh, sorry," she's saying. "I forgot you don't go by 'Brigham' anymore, do you?"

It doesn't feel like she's sorry. It feels like she's stalling. "It's okay," I tell the lady with my mother's voice, "You can call me whatever you want."

The more my aunt speaks, the less she sounds like Mom. Aunt Deb's voice is pitched a bit lower than Mom's and it moves faster – like she's actually aware people might have something else to do besides sit right where they are and listen to her all day. "Well, I'm calling with news. I'm calling to let you know Grandma died."

It's one of those announcements that's supposed to come as

a relief. We're all supposed to pack up our loss in talk about how Grandma was old and sick and ready to move on, or whatever. It is true that, by the end, she couldn't form any new short-term memories. It meant she honestly believed none of us had visited her, there in her nursing home, for years and years. It got so bad Aunt Deb left a Polaroid camera in Grandma's room and had everyone who came to visit take a photo with her and sign their names on a calendar just so they wouldn't have to argue about whether anyone had been there. But then Grandma started coming up with all those conspiracy theories about faked photos and forged signatures. That crazy, crushing loneliness – at least that's over for her, I guess.

The round of phone calls Aunt Deb is making today is different from the one I had to make the night we found Mom face down on her living room carpet. With Grandma, we'd all been able to telegraph this announcement from a long way off. It doesn't come crashing in from the blind side like it did with Mom – but that doesn't mean my grandmother's death is not a shock.

I still have the presence of mind to thank Aunt Deb for handling the funeral arrangements. "It's a lot of work," I say.

"You don't even know," is her answer, even though I do know. And I'm not angry that she's forgotten – not at all, not right now.

Aunt Deb will be on the phone for days, so she wants me to call my brother and sisters to tell them what's happened. She gives me the details of the funeral arrangements. It will be held on Wednesday, in the middle of the workday, in a city where none of my parents' kids live. It's nothing like a convenient time or place, but it's not out of driving range either. Each one of my siblings could make a day trip to get there. Aunt Deb invites me to say a prayer out loud, into a microphone, at the end of the funeral service. I haven't quite finished writing all the funeral particulars down when she tells me goodbye.

I'm sitting down at the kitchen table with the cordless phone in my hand when you come to kiss the top of my head. "I'm sorry, Brigs," you say. "I loved her too."

In a moment, you hand me the address book, knowing there's no way I'll have all my siblings' phone numbers memorized. "Take a few minutes – before you start," you say when I begin flipping through the thumb-tabs of the battered coil-bound book right away. "It's alright if you're not okay."

I nod and let out a long breath through my mouth. But it doesn't help. "I gotta make these calls."

I contact my siblings in their birth order, for some reason. My first sister sighs and sounds properly grave. "Well," she says after a pause. "Grandma led a good, long life. I, for one, am happy for her to be released from mortality."

I think I understand why some people feel it's alright to say stuff like that. But it still makes me want to punch something.

I'm part of the way through telling my sister about the funeral plans when she interrupts. "You're going to be driving down there for it, right, Brigham?"

"Yeah."

"So – if one person comes to represent our side of the family, we're not *all* expected to be there, are we?"

For a second, I can't say anything. It's like I don't even understand what she's said.

"Expected."

I repeat the word once before I default to carrying out Aunt Deb's instructions. I'm like an automated message service meting out the rest of the funeral schedule and quietly hanging up the phone. You're standing beside me again, alarmed by my robotic voice. I repeat what my sister told me and bow my head as you act out my own disgust for me.

"What is the matter with that girl?"

It's easier that way.

The next call is to my other sister, the one who responds to just about every kind of stress by getting mad. I know by now not to take it personally, but it's still hard to face sometimes. I'm not sure if I've called her on the phone since the night after we found Mom dead. It's bad, but maybe my sister is starting to identify my telephone voice as the trump of death, or something like that. I can sense her bristling even before we've finished with our hard, dry hellos.

Naturally, she's angry right away when I tell her about Grandma. "Dangit, Brigham."

"Yeah, I'll miss her too," I try to agree.

"Well, I'd like to go to the funeral. But not everyone can afford to drop everything and fork over a load of money for the gas to get down there."

"Can I give you some money for the gas? I'd like to help."

She yells out a laugh that sounds distinctly insulted though she won't be reckless enough to try to start a fight – not today. Instead she says, "I'll get back to you on that." But I know she won't.

"Let me guess: she's mad," you say when the call is over.

I shrug. "It could have been worse."

The final call is to the brother I only lived with for eight years before I grew up and left for the Philippines, never to live at home with him again. He's the one I can't help feeling like I abandoned – a little brown boy left to himself in the wasteland of our parents' disintegrating marriage. In some ways, he's like a long lost relative of mine, almost a stranger. And then in other ways, he's so close he's like the unofficial fifth son of my marriage to you, even now that he's grown up.

If death is my province of the family, then love is my brother's – voracious, child-like love. Maybe that's why I've never seen in-laws take to each other as easily as he took to you. Even though he was almost as tall as you already, he was still just a kid the first time I brought you home to my family. I can still see him, capering around the car in the bright prairie sunlight as I rolled to a stop under the hollow poplar trees in my parents' front yard. As an adult, my brother looks like me only toasted brown and buffed up for skilled manual labour. But as the child you met that afternoon, he was all knees and elbows and no personal space at all. He darted around you like a Cupid celebrating an emerging Venus – my own mildly heat-exhausted Venus, stepping out of the car and onto the grass.

For the first time in all of today's death knelling, you come and stand still, right there at my side – all pain and tension – as I dial my brother's number into the phone. The only contact information we have for him is a cell phone number that hardly ever connects.

"It'll be a miracle if you can get him to pick it up," you say.

And maybe that's just what it is. My brother answers his phone. He answers it even though he's at work. I can hear the air compressors that power his pneumatic tools pounding up the pressure in the background. It doesn't matter. He keeps still while I tell him what's happened to our grandmother and then he starts to bawl – right on the jobsite, right into the phone. It's awful. It's even worse than when I called to tell him about Mom melting into the floor of her trailer. There was never any ambivalence in my brother's love for our grandmother. She never hurt him, disappointed him, left him – not like Mom. This death of Grandma's – there's no relief in it for him, no vindication, just grief. On the other end of the phone, our Cupid is crashing in a heap of feathers and arrows.

I'm pinching the bridge of my nose, the pads of my fingers dammed against the tear ducts in the corners of my eyes. "I'm so sorry," I tell him.

He can't speak but I hear him struggling – all breath and tears – miles and miles away. And somehow, you know it all even though you can't hear any of it. You're leaning over me at the kitchen table while I've still got the phone held to my ear. Everyone knows angels lost their wings ages ago – back in the Renaissance, I'm pretty sure. We've outgrown the need for them ourselves and we're each left with two arms in their place. You fold yours around my shoulders. They draw me against you. And you're whispering my little brother's name like a warm, wet prayer, your face pressed into the side of my neck.

## Eleven

You're sitting with your father, looking out at the winter darkness from inside the frosted windows of his car. The heater is roaring in the dash, and you're parked in a vast, empty, snowdrifted parking lot outside a closed-up shopping mall. The two of you are eating cheeseburgers out of foil paper and drinking diet cola through straws by the light of the neon signs overhead – because as far as either of you know, that's love.

It's been days and days since you've last talked to your father like this – not since before he bundled your splotchy, teary mother onto an airplane and took her to her father's funeral, far away, in New Brunswick, on the east coast of this huge, frozen country. It was the funeral of your last surviving grandfather – the one you were raised to call "Grampy" – the one who died shovelling heavy, wet, Maritime snow off the roof of his little red brick house. They're still not sure if he fell off the roof and then had a heart attack or had a heart attack and then fell off the roof. I guess it never really mattered.

At age nineteen, you were left at home with your strange little heap of grief and your mob of younger brothers while both your parents were gone across the continent. It wasn't an easy assignment, but you thought you were coping well. That was before your sweetie-pie German professor stopped you in the doorway as you left her classroom to ask if everything was alright. She told you to stay behind and offered you a cup of peppermint tea and the chance to talk to someone about your Opa. All that German tenderness – your Grampy wasn't the kind of old World War II soldier who would have still found it ironic. He understood about duty and reconciliation and how the universe needs to operate.

"So the funeral service was nice, eh?" you ask your Dad in the cold car.

He nods into the paper wrapped around his hamburger. "It was fine," he agrees. "At the luncheon afterwards, your grandmother's cousin called me fat right to my face – but she meant no harm. They never do. It's just what I've learned to expect when I go among people like your mother's – people 'in whom there is no guile.'"

It makes you smile.

"Really," he continues. "Did you know they call their town's cemetery site 'Butcher Hill'?"

You laugh. "No, I was not aware of that."

Your dad shakes his head. "They don't mean to be morbid, and I'm sure they have some perfectly innocent explanation for it. They always do."

You nod. "No one out there's trying to make it sound ghoulish on purpose."

"Yeah, your mother's family are good people." He's nodding too. He means what he says. Even when his in-laws don't seem very good, he knows by now to give them the benefit of the doubt. "Yes, the indoor parts of the funeral were all fine. But the weather outside – the weather was – awful."

"Mom was saying the same thing. But that's February in the Maritimes for ya, right?"

"No." His voice is low and grave. "It wasn't just the season. It was – *awful*."

"Awful." You hold tightly to your paper cup and you wait.

Your Dad begins to tell you how freezing rain was falling all over the region for days before and after your grandfather's funeral. Ice coated all the cars until buckets of hot water had to be carried out and poured over their doors to melt the ice sheets long enough to get them open. And all of Butcher Hill, right up to your grandfather's graveside, was coated in thick, glossy hummocks of slick, new ice. It was constantly washed in cold water from the rain still driving at the land, coming in sideways from the Atlantic Ocean to the east.

"Wet ice," he says. "There's nothing slipperier than that – not even in the Maritimes."

He tells you how even with all the road-salt caked over everything, the tires of the funeral cortege abandoned their usual solemnity and screamed against the icy hillside – the long black cars swaying back and forth, all the way up Butcher Hill on the narrow cemetery road.

He pauses to comfort himself with a sip from his straw before he tells you about the procession of pallbearers. They came forward in their raincoats, sliding over the wet ice toward the grave, the casket pitching between them like a badly made boat as they lost and found their footing, over and over again.

*Jennifer Quist*

"They're all slipping around in leather-soled fancy dress shoes – no traction at all."

And your Dad waited with your mother under the umbrellas the funeral home lent them, standing near the lip of the open grave. Everyone watched – gasping, frowning, praying – as the pallbearers made the slow, tortured trek over the ice.

"Everyone was looking at the pall bearers. And maybe that's why no one noticed – not a single one of them noticed – that the bottom of the grave itself was full of ice-water. No one noticed besides me, I mean."

Your grandfather's grave was a meat locker machine-cut out of the frozen mud of Butcher Hill. And in the bottom of the hole, a full foot of brown water lay pocked with the ever-falling ice rain while your father, helpless, waited for something unspeakable to happen.

In the car, the two of you are staring out the windshield, straight ahead, as if your grandfather's burial scene is playing where you can't help but see it on the dirty glass in front of your faces.

"So they're coming across the ice with the casket – holding onto those pretty metal bars with both hands, their feet slipping and tripping all over the place. And I keep going from gaping at the funeral director to the minister they borrowed from the local United Church and then back into the grave-water. I have no idea what to do."

"No, of course not."

"So I didn't do anything."

"That's fine, Daddy. It's fine." But you're already choking.

"Inside that box was my wife's father, all freshly washed and

100

dressed and – clean. I'd just seen him for myself in the church at the foot of the hill. And we'd all whispered and acted like he was something holy and then – then – *don't put him in the water*."

"Just – just try to think of it as a burial at sea," you offer.

Your Dad coughs, nodding. "Yeah. Anyway, the pallbearers made it to the grave – though I had to grab your Uncle Ray by his coattails to keep him from sliding into the hole as he set his corner of the coffin down on the straps."

"Poor Uncle Ray."

"Yes, poor Uncle Ray," he sighs.

Then it's quiet in the car. The scene on the windshield isn't moving anymore. The coffin stands in the ice-rain over the grave. It's right at the back of the cemetery where the avenue of dwarf blue spruces standing against the barbed wire fence is so laden in ice it looks like every needle has been crafted out of glass. The waterlogged grave is open, waiting.

You hear your father swallow. "And then, as if it was a perfect spring morning, they lowered it – flipped a switch and the machinery hummed away and the eight thousand dollar glossy, golden oak casket sank into the water, with him still inside it. Just when he must have thought he couldn't get any colder..."

And the scene on the windshield changes from a rainy hillside to darkness – just darkness with the rush of cold, cold water through the hinges and clasps and tiny breaches in the heavily lacquered wood and the white satin upholstery.

You close your eyes but the image stays with you until you shake your head. You're mouthing words to yourself. "Burial at sea."

When you speak out loud, your throat is dry and tight.

"Mom didn't see – did she?"

Your Dad shakes his head. "Honestly, I don't know. And how can I ever ask her about it now?"

You shrug against the stiff vinyl of the car's passenger seat. The cold air has crept into your nose and you sniff against it. Your Dad hears and turns to see you.

"I'm sorry, honey," he says, crumpling his handful of greasy foil paper and jamming it into a waste-bag on the floor at your feet. "Maybe I was wrong to make you hear all that."

"No, no. Not if it makes you feel any better to talk about it."

"It doesn't. I should know that already. It never does."

And it's true, what they told you in your classes at the university – in the vast lecture theatres full of young adult hubris and lingering teen-aged angst. When it comes to human happiness, catharsis, they taught you, is one of the oldest lies we have.

"No." Your Dad knows. "No, telling doesn't help a dang."

It doesn't make any difference that you agree with him. In the dark of the parking lot, inside the cold glass and steel of the car, you close your eyes. You let your hands rest on the tops of your thighs, upturned, your fingers relaxed into curves like rows of crescent moons. And you breathe in through your nose, so deeply that your head tips back against the seat of the car. You draw in the same air your father moved with the sound of his story – sucking it into yourself. You pull it so far into your own body that your ribs strain and your throat aches around it, crushing from the inside with the pressure of it all. And then – you let it go.

# Twelve

You've got nothing but hard, narrow eyes for the funeral director when the time comes to go east again, to New Brunswick, to bury Grampy's wife. She's your last grandmother, the one you all called "Nanny." The funeral director's feelings don't mean much to me but still I hope he doesn't hear you calling him the "rented funeral man." In the Butcher Hill Cemetery, you poke me with your elbow to make sure I notice that his black suit is all glassy in the sun – like he left the iron sitting for too long on that polyester blend. You're right – the thing's half melted. But I won't agree with you when you try to tell me how he must save his better suits for better families.

Thousands of miles from home, we've stepped out of the car (which really is rented) and into a cemetery where there are hardly any graves that aren't connected to your family in some way. It's funny, for once, to be somewhere I'm the stranger and you're the not-quite-unfamiliar face in a huge, old clan.

Here in the cemetery, near the crest of Butcher Hill, there's no rain, no ice, and we can see the blue shingled roof of the house in the valley where your Grampy and Nanny used to live. I'm just about to make sure you notice the view when I find you're all agitated again, huffing about how the rented funeral man has thrown down a mat of plastic turf-junk right over your Grampy's headstone. It's too bad. Who did he think would already be buried in the plot adjacent to the one where we're making Nanny's grave today? Thanks to my mother, you've planned a funeral before, and you won't be cowed by the officiousness of it all – not anymore. You step right up to the edge of the plastic turf.

"He's right here. Look, I'll show you," you say to me.

But you aren't quite bold enough to keep from glancing behind yourself to see if the rented funeral man is watching. You're tugging upward on the frayed edge of the turf, folding the green plastic garbage-carpet off the bones of your ancestors. There it is, just like you said it would be: your Grampy's headstone, planted there over the grave your father watched filling up with ice water, years and years ago. I wonder if it ever thawed out and drained away. Maybe your grandfather is sealed up in a dirty brown ice cube in the ground beneath our feet, like a cave man caught in a glacier. Maybe he's a natural cryogenic wonder, frozen in the earth just as perfect as the day he fell off the blue roof and into the snow.

"I love how his headstone is so elegant and simple," you say, defying the prejudices of no one in particular. "Remember that when you're ordering one for me, Brigs. I don't want anything too fussy – no statues of angels or lambs."

"I thought gravestone lambs were just for dead babies."

You're turning away from me, waving one hand. "Everyone's the same age in heaven."

Now you want me to tell you if the rented funeral man looked our way while you were bent over. I don't know so you give me your elbow again and tell me to watch him next time. You know he sees you. You're hard to miss, standing with the wind blowing all your long hair straight up over your head like a stringy, yellow torch.

"Oh, come on," I say when you complain about what the wind's done to your hair. "What's a funeral on Butcher Hill without a good hurricane blowing?"

You laugh – because this is an airy, churchy funeral, after all, and laughing is just fine. "Is it wind," you ask, "or is it more like suction? Like someone left the door cracked between here and the Spirit World, and it's all we can do not to get siphoned right inside."

Whatever it is, your Nanny's coffin sure looks rickety out here in all this wind. The box isn't exactly the top of the line model. Your Mom's older sisters, the ladies you call "the Aunties" told us how mad Nanny was about the prices of the coffins in the showroom the day she picked this one out. They say she took one of the fancy, folded price tags – written in calligraphy like a place card at a posh banquet – snatched it right off the pillow inside a coffin, and threw it down on the floor where she could stomp on it.

"For heck's sake, it's a casket, not a coffin," the Aunties correct each other. "Coffins are for vampires. And she was no vampire."

But the word leaves you wincing. "I just hate the sound of it – 'casket.' Something about it makes me think of shucking corn or – the dry insect egg casings you find in the dust when

105

you wash out the light fixtures in the fall."

The Aunties roll their eyes at you. "This one was always Nanny's pet."

I think all of them – your grandmother and the Aunties following her around the casket showroom with the funeral pre-planning worksheet tacked to a clipboard – must have found something to enjoy in the ugly little scene. Nanny got to rage, rage right up against the dying of the light. And all her quiet, furious objections about how expensive everything was going to be in the end just seemed kind of cute to her daughters.

"None of it's negotiable, Mom. There's no point getting your shirt in a knot over it."

At one point, the legend says, Nanny told the Aunties just to bury her in one of the rough alder wood crates the caskets are packed into before they're shipped out of the factory. Everyone laughed, even though they knew she wasn't joking.

So this wind-whipped casket standing out here on Butcher Hill is the bargain-basement model, just like she wanted. The Aunties say, when the family's not around, the funeral people will refer to her casket as "the Pink Pauper" model. I don't know about that, but the casket is pink, all right. The fibre-board it's made out of is covered with a rough salmon-coloured brocade fabric – like it's meant to look like a battered old skin, I guess. The funeral people trade in shame. Maybe they want us to think about how burial in a bargain casket is just a hair's breadth better than getting thrown into the ground bare naked.

And they warned Nanny the lid of a casket like this one would collapse under the weight of the grave's own dirt. It might be true but it won't matter here – not in a county cemetery governed by bylaws that demand every casket be sealed in concrete at the bottom of every new grave. I guess the county must be afraid its dead might end up seeping into the ground-water or something, accidentally fertilizing hay fields or mak-ing the earthworms a little too human or – I don't know what. "Grave liner" is what the concrete's called on funeral man's in-voice. I think it's actually the cheapest thing on there.

The grave liner is on your mind too. "When do they put in the – the concrete?" you ask the Aunties from behind your hand. It's the first sign of shame I've seen from you all day – the first thing to break through your façade of bossy frenzy.

The Aunties nod toward the hole in the ground. "The con-crete? It's already here."

You make the tiniest perceptible stagger backward. "What? How can it be here already? We didn't even put the coffin down there yet. There's nothing for them to pour it over."

Then the Aunties are laughing at you – quietly, in snorts and muffled gasps because, church funeral or not, we are at the open edge of their mother's grave.

"What in the world do you mean, dear?"

We cremated my mother, slipping her already sealed and sanitary into the earth, so you and I have never had to deal with burial by concrete before. I look at you as you wait for the Aunties to stop laughing. You're standing with your lips open and your eyes wide and watery blue. And I think I might know better now, more than ever before, how you must have looked when you were a child.

"They don't pack her in wet cement," the Aunties tell you, wiping their eyes. "When they say concrete they just mean a dry, pre-formed empty concrete box with a big, heavy lid – "

" – like a crypt, only under the ground."

"Yes. A little, secret tomb within the grave."

Your hand clamps over one of the Auntie's arms while you look into the face of the other Auntie. "Did Nanny know that?"

The Aunties look at each other. One of them shrugs. The other shakes her head as she says, "I can't imagine how she wouldn't have known."

"Now dear, you don't think she was expecting us to back a cement mixer right up to her open grave and – "

"Beep, beep, beep." The Aunties are laughing again as they imitate the back-up warning signal of a heavy-duty cement truck.

"Well," you interrupt as best you can, "that's what I always thought everyone meant when they talked about burying her in concrete. So maybe she – why else would she have been so mad about it?"

One of the Aunties pats your hand where it grips her sleeve. "No, dear. Of course they don't mean wet cement. Go see for yourself," she tells you. "In the bottom of the grave – the concrete box is down there already. Go take a look – carefully."

And you're bent over again only this time you truly don't care who is watching or what they might see. I step up behind you to try to keep the wind out of your skirt as you lean low enough to see beneath the casket strung on a nest of nylon straps over the open grave.

"There it is, Brigs," you say, almost in a moan. "That's all it is – a grey box just slightly bigger than the coffin itself." You straighten up but you don't stand back. "She must not have understood – the same way I didn't understand. I mean, did you ever hear of her getting madder about anything in her whole life than the thought of burial by concrete? I tried, the Aunties tried, Mom tried, we all tried to settle her down but she just kept imagining herself on the morning of the resurrection, perfect and whole and sealed up in solid concrete forever. How's that for eternal life?"

You're standing up, leaving me, moving to work the crowd. "Have you seen it yet?" you say, shaking your cousins by their arms. "Don't leave here before you see the concrete grave liner stronger than the Resurrection."

You move through the crowd, threading through the small spaces between all the bodies, coming back to me, smiling and taking my hand again. "It's just a box, Brigs — just another, bigger, stronger, uglier box."

"So it is."

"And of course she'll find her way out of it."

"Of course."

But just as quickly as you took hold of my hand, you let it go again. "I've got to send something with her — just in case."

This time you go all the way down on your knees beside the grave.

"Come on. That's enough," I say.

Is anyone even looking? Is the rented funeral man so used to the sight of you poking around, in and out of this grave, that he's beyond doing anything but rolling his eyes.

I whisper your name and bend over you like a shield. My fingers are laced through the loose black weave of your cardigan, barely tugging you backward. It's too much. You've got to get up.

But you've inserted your face into the gap between the open

earth and the coffin hovering in the air above it. And out of your small, warm mouth – there, one ribbon of saliva. Look, it's already supernova-ed on the floor of the concrete box and shot into the tiny pores between all that well-cured cement. Even from outside the grave, we can see where the concrete's stained dark with your water and enzymes – the same ones that make the yoghurt go all watery when you eat it right out of the tub and put it back in the fridge. There it is, already dissolving your grandmother's tomb. There'll be nothing on the rented funeral man's invoice to show you falling fast behind her – landing with a splat and whatever faith she lacks.

Even after the argument with your Mom where she tried to convince you the healthy, life-affirming benefits of letting people see our kids at the funeral would outweigh the cost and the agony of flying them all the way across country, we left the boys behind. They've stayed in the west, at Aunt Marla's house, while we've gone to New Brunswick for Nanny's funeral. This is what it takes for us to make our first trip alone since before the boys were born.

As we were leaving, driving away from Aunt Marla's house, moving down the broad streets of that small town where Mom died, you were all fretful and slumped against the window of the car. "I don't know, Brigs. Benny's still in diapers and everything. I can't believe we're leaving them here."

I knew your reluctance was real but I also knew there was no way we'd turn the car around. Your Aunties had already asked you to speak at Nanny's funeral. Ever since that eulogy you gave at Mom's funeral, you always get asked to stand up at the very end and speak for the dead. And now, there's no way you'd tell any of them "no."

Despite the Aunties' claim that you were Nanny's pet grand-daughter, you know her only through years of birthday cards stuffed with old paper dollar bills – that and one long summer stay by yourself, and the few cross-country road trips that could be arranged during your lifetime. But Nanny is yours, nonetheless. You're easy about accepting and multiplying real though implausible love – so easy you don't even realize it's a gift.

Now, in the afternoon after Nanny's funeral, we're out of our mourning clothes and into pairs of borrowed, leaky gum-boots and heavy, red-checked lumberjack shirts. We're tramp-ing through the woods between the swift brown river and the old house where Nanny used to live when she was a little girl. It's too early in the season for blackflies, so the forest is wet but not unpleasant. It's all mist and quiet in here, and you're calling to me through the stillness of the soggy trees, telling me how you and your brothers passed the time on those long, coast-to-coast car rides playing Go Fish with postcards you'd collected.

"Do you have any 'Moncton's Magnetic Hill: Canada's Third Greatest Natural Wonder?'"

"Nope. Go fish."

In these woods, you're acting bold and well-oriented, but I know it's mostly just noise and bravado. You've been here many times before, but these are still not quite your woods. The trees crowd the ground around this Maritime river differ-ently than they do in the scanty stands of trees on the prairies where we grew up.

Nanny's forest is close and canopied but there's room for

111

us to walk between the long trunks of the deciduous trees. I keep plucking maple leaves, eyeing them like I'm going to press them in books and keep them forever – even though you're laughing at me.

"What?" I protest. "Maple leaves are cool. They don't grow wild back home."

Ahead of me, you stop walking and look around us. It kind of freaks me out, the way we know this forest spreads to the very edges of the continental landmass where the earth is worn away to bedrock and butted onto the sea. In the light filtered by the leafy trees, spruces grow out of the moss in tightly spiked copses and let their sap stand out on their trunks in yellowed, purple knobs. You tell me people used to pick the sap and chew it up like gum. But when I dare you to show me, all you do is get close enough to notice the spruce gum is actually covered in tiny spider webs. After that, you won't even touch it.

And I know what the real difference is between these trees and the ones I know from the west. These ones are more human, less wild. Centuries before people like my ancestors were anywhere near the prairies, these woods had already snagged and held small traces of settled, human life. There are still wet remains of old foot bridges across streams, or flaky red nails rusting where they have been pounded into tree trunks and bent over for some long-forgotten purpose. The forests here have overgrown and outlasted generations of families like ours. All the history makes the place heavy with your ancestors' lives and deaths. It's like they've left an imprint here you can almost sense – like you're just on the verge of remembering something.

And we are trying to remember something. The Aunties

112

say there's an old family cemetery out here somewhere – the place where your grandmother would have been buried in an alder wood crate, without a cement liner, if the county still allowed it. Instead, she's buried up on Butcher Hill in the "new" cemetery. The new cemetery was started just in time to receive the nine of your great-great- grandmother's eleven children who died in an influenza epidemic still known by the old-timers around here as "The Black Death."

"Yep," you'll rasp out of bed at me at least once during the course of every flu you ever get. "It's true. I come from a long line of miserable Scottish people who coughed themselves to death."

Influenza isn't what scares you out here in the woods today. You tell me how the last time you traipsed around here looking for the old graveyard, you were just a kid terrified of your Mom's canon of true, family ghost stories – stories you're repeating to me now, as we walk over the moss, side by side but metres apart, like a search-and-rescue party.

"And as they ran, they could hear old Sarah – off in the distance, always ahead of them – waving her blue-white light and justa screamin' in the dead of night."

I think it's funny how you start to take on their Maritime accents more and more with every hour we stay here. But I don't mention it now. Instead, I just laugh as the ghost story ends. "You don't scare me."

"That," you say, "is only because you've never been out here at night. There's no light at all in the woods after the sun goes down – nothing. It's like being locked in a closet with nothing but spruce trees hanging from the rod."

"I don't know." I'm a little bit worried about you, so I'm

trying to sound sceptical. "I guess I don't find trees that spooky. It's just a bunch of wood planted in the ground, right? It'd be like being afraid of the dining room furniture, wouldn't it?"

I hear your scoffing sound. "It's not the trees themselves. It's what's in them – all the ghosts and shadows and stuff. And I still say it's easy to be cavalier about it in the daytime. When the sun's up even these old graveyards are just part of the Earth. You know – like any features on the landscape."

I stop and scan the terrain around us. "Well, where is the graveyard then?" I'm starting to get a soaker in the toe of my gumboot.

You're not answering my question. "Hey, check it out." You're bending down and picking a little oval leaf off a twig growing out of a low, hollow spot in the moss that covers everything.

I squint down at the groundcover. "Kinnikinnick?"

"No. They're teaberry leaves."

I've never heard of teaberry leaves, but you're rubbing the dirt off them and putting the leaves right into your mouth anyway.

"Come on, Brigs. You're supposed to be the mighty forager in the family. Try a teaberry leaf. It beats the heck out of your lame prairie chokecherries. Trust me." You pluck a leaf for me. It's tiny and kind of disappears between my teeth when I bite it. The taste is strong and hot – like sandy wintergreen toothpaste spread on a twig.

I'm nodding. "Sure. It's nice."

But you're grabbing me by the waist with both of your hands. "You didn't swallow it, did you?"

I sweep the cavern of my mouth with my tongue. "Yeah, I think I did."

"Brigs!"

"What? Don't tell me you just got me to put something in my mouth that you didn't expect me to eat."

"Well – yeah. I mean, teaberry leaves are like spruce gum. You aren't supposed to swallow them, you big animal."

"Why not?"

"I – I don't know. Nanny never told us it was okay to swallow the leaves whole so – I don't know."

You're looking up at me with the little girl face from the funeral again – all wild with the terrifying superstitions from the Stone Age of your childhood.

I pull your hands off my torso and pile them on top of each other in my palm. "I'm fine," I say. "I'm going to stay fine."

You're trotting after me as I walk away from the teaberry patch. "Are you sure?"

I hold out my arms. "Look at the size of me. One little leaf's not going to hurt me – even if there is a possibility that they aren't so good for eating."

You cross your arms and purse your lips. "So spit out the rest of the saliva left in your mouth."

"Come on…"

"Brigs – please. Get rid of it. Please."

I turn my head and spit onto the ground. You jump up to kiss me on the cheek as I wipe my lips with the back of my hand.

"Thanks, Sweetie."

I breathe out a noisy sigh. "Back to grave hunting, okay?"

"Right." You nod and start to walk again. "Remember: we're looking for stones stood on their narrow ends, set in a group – like a small, haphazard Stonehenge."

"Not like that?" I say, pointing back into the grove where we just stood chewing teaberry leaves.

And then you're crashing past me, stomping over the twiggy vines, back into the open space in the trees where flat sheets of natural, ragged-edged shale – nothing like Stonehenge – stand on their ends, half buried in the ground. The earth in front of each of the stones bows down in long rectangles the size of small graves – the size of you. At least five of the shale monoliths stand in the glade, reverently apart from one another – uncut headstones pried raw from the earth and set in unnatural positions by people who are long gone. You stoop and scan their surfaces, but there's nothing written on the stones – nothing that can still be read, anyways. So instead of looking any further, you stand up straight and you listen as if you're trying to read something in the low, spiritual hum you so badly want to hear resonating though the forgotten boneyard. You look up through the trees, straight above us, where a flat white sky spreads like a drab, painted ceiling overhead.

"Do you see Caroline anywhere?" you ask me. "Lost Caroline?"

I know you mean the grave of your great-grandmother's aunt – or someone like that. She's what someone might try to call a "romantic" figure. She was a young mother – just a newly married teenager, really – buried somewhere in the ground out here with a tiny son still closed between her arms. We were warned that her grave wouldn't have a natural marker hacked out of shale or wood but a real milled granite one – smooth and symmetrical and modern. They say Caroline's stepson – one of the many of them born years after Caroline's death, the children of her husband's strong, new wife – had replaced her handmade, wooden cross with a real granite monument. Everyone said it was silly but the stepson was a prosperous person who could afford to be sentimental.

I step into the grove with you, combing all the wet bracken into a kind of flatness with the side of my boot. As I knock the ferns down, it comes into view – the machine cut stone lying out of time and place in the moss.

"Here she is."

You're hopping over the undergrowth to see for yourself. "Here she is," you repeat, taking my hand in yours. But you let go of me again before I can close my fingers around your flesh and bones – just like you did at your grandmother's graveside this morning. You're about to revise another burial – the second one of the day – no matter how late it might be for Lost Caroline.

There's a thin, creamy birch trunk – no leaves, no branches – standing dead and jutting at a forty-five degree angle out of the moss. You kick at its base and the trunk snaps off so easily you nearly fall down right along with it.

"Help me break it into pieces," you tell me, carrying the trunk to where I still stand over Lost Caroline and her baby.

The wood snaps easily into short lengths when we crack it over our knees. "What now?" I ask.

You hesitate, standing over the pile of white, broken wood. "Her headstone – it's nice but it doesn't quite belong here. Everyone says so but no one will do anything to try to salvage it. It just needs – something," you say.

There's another pause – a long one. "Do you want to mark

117

it with a cross – the way they would have originally marked it right after they buried her?" I venture.

It's a difficult question. You squint, furrowing your forehead, shifting your mouth to one side of your face. The truth is we'd no sooner use a cross to refer to anything heavenly than we'd use a Nazi machine gun shell to commemorate our great-uncles who were killed in the war.

It's what you're thinking right now as you say, "Caroline didn't die on a cross." Your face softens and you look up at the flat, white sky again. "She died – all torn up in love for this baby and his father."

I let my hand fall, cupping your shoulder.

You drop to kneel on Lost Caroline's grave even though the downward force of your weight wrings water out of the mossy earth. It soaks through your clothes, all the way to the skin on your shins and kneecaps. You're laying down the lengths of broken birch wood – piece by piece.

I squat beside you. "What are we making?" At first, you don't answer, but you don't stop laying the wood down either. It's starting to form into a shape like a tight curve. "Are you making her initial: a letter C?"

"No, Brigs. We are marking this grave," you tell me, "with a wedding ring."

We get back to the house of the Auntie we're staying with – a photo of Lost Caroline's headstone stored in the memory of my cell phone. Our plane leaves from the Fredericton International Airport in a few hours, so it's time to dry our feet and get ready to leave. The trip from here to the airport should only take a little over an hour but everyone else in the house is getting fussy and acting like it's a long way. I guess one hour's traffic is a lot, here in a tiny Maritime county.

I'm zipping my black suit into a garment bag when I catch you sitting on the edge of the bed, stalled, with a sock dangling from each of your hands.

"Auntie sure keeps it warm in here," you say when you see me looking at you.

I frown and cover your forehead with the palm of my hand. Your skin is dry and hot. "You're sick."

You clamp your hand over mine. "No."

"Don't tell me you swallowed your teaberry leaves."

You almost smile. "No. That's not it."

"Then you must be coming down with a virus or something."

"But I can't be sick. What if someone at the airport notices I've got a fever and they won't let me on the plane?"

I don't even shrug. "They'll let you on the plane."

You're pulling your socks on quickly now, as if hurrying will help. "But they have all those pandemics going around these days. What if someone decides I've got SARS or bird flu or something?"

I laugh. "SARS? That was ages ago."

"So? We need to get back to the kids tonight. Aunt Marla's been too generous already. We need to get the boys out of her house." You look around the room from where you're still slumped on the edge of the bed. "I need to find some medicine to take before we try to board the plane."

I go to the house's single bathroom and bring back one tab-

119

let of the only fever reducing drug Auntie has in her medicine cabinet. She told me they're left over from the hernia surgery she had last year, and we're welcome to take them all. I won't tell you that. The pills are those acetaminophen tablets with codeine added to them. I shake one out of the bottle and close the rest of them back inside the cabinet. Medication like this always knocks me right out. But as soon as you see me coming through the bedroom door with the lone tablet in the palm of my hand you're sending me back for more.

"Are you trying to insult me or something? Brigs, you know my liver has super powers. I need more than one pill."

I come back, squinting at the writing curving along the surface of the pill bottle. "Look, it says here not to exceed – "

You stand up – fast, like you're much more angry than you are sick. "Well, my family's past generations of super-metabolizing alcoholics say otherwise – "

"You're invoking all those coughing, dead alcoholics – now?"

"Yes."

I stand back, holding the plastic pill bottle over my head, well out of your reach. "Lamarck was wrong, you know," I argue. "You can't inherit the drug tolerance your ancestors acquired over lifetimes of hard drinking – especially when you've never even tasted alcohol yourself."

You're clawing at my sleeve, trying to climb up my arm, toward the bottle. "Of course I know that, Brigs. I never claimed I had my ancestors' drug tolerance." You make a weak little jump for my hand. "What I did inherit is their super-liver – the liver so awesome they had to drink enough to bring on an addiction before they could even feel a buzz."

"But don't you have a grandmother who has an allergic reaction to heavy meds?"

You jump a little higher this time. "That is the *other* side of the family. The one I don't take after."

"You don't know that for sure."

"I do so."

I still won't lower my arm.

"Come on, it's not like Auntie's pills are hard drugs or anything," you say. "If you want, I'll promise to go right into rehab without any complaining as soon as we land back home. Please..."

Knowing I can't keep the pills from you forever, I give in. You swallow the first tablet without any water so I go get you a glass and stand watching as you down the second dose. I wonder if they'll let us onto the plane if I arrive at the gate carrying you over my shoulder like deadweight.

The drugs are powerful enough to get your fever down. And even though your eyes are disappearing into the dark circles beneath your brows, you still sit beside me in the rented car crowing, "I told you. Do I seem stoned to you? Do I?" You press your hands against the bottom edge of your ribcage, the space where your liver must be. "Super powers!"

By the time we both walk onto the plane you've stopped proclaiming your super powers but you still haven't fallen to sleep. We take our seats over the wing and I can't tell if it's the drugs, or exhaustion, or just affection that prompts you to let your head droop against the side of my arm. Through the fabric of my shirt, I can feel your skin starting to burn again. You stay that way until there's no ocean outside my airplane window anymore – there are hardly even any lakes. There are

121

just brown and green squares, rectangles, and other perfect polygons – the working fields cultivated all over the prairies. No one has to tell me we're almost home.

"I wish you said my name more often," you murmur with super-heated breath against my arm.

"Your name?"

"Yeah. It would be nice to hear my name more – my real name, I mean. The one my parents gave me, not the one the kids gave me."

I turn my head and press my closed mouth into the heat of your crown. "You need to sleep." When I inhale, your hair smells like that enormous bottle of wheat germ and honey shampoo from your Auntie's bathroom. On you, it's sweet.

You're scorching more speech against my arm. "I just had a weird little half-awake dream. You weren't in it though. I was by myself and I was rising out of this dark space, breaking through tangled up tree roots with my body, all laid out flat. And there was something closed between my arms but they were so stiff I couldn't tell what it was. And then there was this rush of really pungent – something – like black forest loam sifting over my face. And when I broke through I knew it was, like, pine needles and the lobes of spruce cones and dry, empty insect shells. I was coming up out of the earth and someone was calling me. Someone was calling me – Caroline."

# Thirteen

Your cousin Janae's wedding was one of those lavish pink fantasy weddings, the kind mothers insist on for daughters who get married right out of high school just in case the brides never accomplish anything else worth a big party during the rest of their lives. You're well out of high school but still single when Janae marries that guy even though he's so much older than her. Word in the family is that you've read something in one of your university textbooks about destructive power imbalances between spouses with wide gaps between their ages. But the family agrees all that intellectual mumbo-jumbo of yours is just a smoke screen to hide the fact that you're lovelorn, at age twenty.

Janae punishes you for their talk by not inviting you to stand beside her at the wedding reception wearing a pale pink satin dress that will look like it's made of tin foil in all the flash photography. So here you are, playing the Cinderella of the wedding. You're too estranged from the bride to be an overdressed member of the wedding party with a free manicure and a new pair of shoes. But you're still close enough to her to work until after midnight tacking pink streamers to the walls of the church hall.

When the glass bowls of pink lemonade punch are full and the trays of after-dinner sweets are piled high enough, you drift away from the wedding reception and onto the burgundy sofa in the foyer outside the hall. This foyer is where we meet.

The first time I see you, the front of your plain black dress is wet across the middle from the time you've spent leaning against the sink, washing the dishes from Janae's "head table" – the only table not set with paper plates. Your black shoes are just like the ones china dolls wear right out of their boxes – round-toed, flat-heeled, with one strap slung across the top of the foot and buckled on the other side.

"Just call them 'Mary Janes,'" you'll tell me much later, when I'm your husband and I miss those shoes and I'm trying to tell you how much I liked them.

At Janae's wedding reception, your Mary Janes lay about a metre apart on the floor of the church foyer. You kicked them off without undoing the buckles before you sat down and pulled your sore feet up underneath yourself. That friend of yours is with you – the girl you share an apartment with during university. Right now, she's better than a sister to you.

"Look at how wet you got in there. You should have let me wash and you could have dried for a while," she chides you.

You just shrug. "Then we'd both be soggy. And there's no point in that."

Your friend is a wholesome, kind, and pretty girl. You're right to love her the way you do. And even though it's almost more embarrassing than I can stand, your nice roommate is the reason I've come here tonight.

Janae doesn't know me yet. Neither does her new husband. I haven't been formally invited to the wedding reception at all. But here I am anyway, in the foyer with the pretty girl and her shoeless friend – the friend wearing a wet dress and argyle knee socks that don't quite stay up. I am the awkward guest-of-a-guest. I've come with my cousin. He's a friend of the groom's and he couldn't be more sure that your pretty roommate is the perfect girl for me – perfect enough, anyways.

She is good-looking, just like my cousin promised me. She's got huge dark eyes like a big game animal – a pretty animal, don't get me wrong. Maybe this is where you got the idea I prefer brunettes. Even though you always laugh through the words, I still hate it when you pull that old line on me. I thought you got an A in that demography seminar you took. Didn't you? If you did, then you should know that most of the people in the world have dark hair so it stands to reason that most of the girls I dated before you would have had dark hair too. No matter how many times I explain it, you keep teasing me about having a "thing" for brunettes.

I've been sticking to the fringes of Janae's wedding reception all evening – still a little sheepish about being here. I walk the circular corridor around the chapel and the main hall, fingering the pink ribbon tied in ringlets around a tiny piece of gift-wrapped fruitcake someone handed to me from a big white basket. It smells spicy but sad – like the week after Christmas, and the disappointment that comes with knowing the good sweets have all been eaten and there won't be any more.

When I see you and your roommate on the burgundy sofa, I have to force myself to sit down. I'm peering around you, looking past you, to the pretty animal on the opposite end. After spending the past two years of my life in the rural Philippines, I can't remember what it is I'm supposed to say to girls like the two of you.

It's okay. You're starting to talk to me first, waving at the piece of fruitcake in my hand. "You're not going to eat that." It isn't a question.

"Why not? I mean, it looks fancy – kinda like it's not really meant for eating. But still…." The words are coming easily. I'm trying not to look surprised at the sound of my own voice.

"Oh, it's edible, alright," you say. "Don't let the ribbon curls scare you."

I smirk. "Yeah, and they must have gone to a lot of trouble to find this ribbon – and all the rest of these decorations in this same, washed-out pink colour."

I don't know it was you who dragged a scissor blade along every shred of this pink ribbon to make all these long curls. Janae set the basket of wrapped cakes in front of you last night, calling it "groom's cake" and promising that if you slept with a piece of it under your pillow on the night of the wedding, you'd dream of the man you were going to marry. I don't know any of it.

You're shaking your head. "You'd better not call it pink. It is not pink. It's 'blush.'"

I can hear something dark in your laugh. "Blush," I repeat. And I'm still a fool so I ask, "How did you guys wind up stuck here doing dishes tonight?"

Your pretty roommate finally speaks. "I came with her." She's poking you with her elbow.

"And I came with my cousin," you add. "She's the bride."

I sit on the church sofa choking apologies for trash-talking the wedding decorations to the bride's cousin. But you act like this kind of mistake is exactly what you want from me. You laugh, loudly, and reach out to drop a small hand very lightly and briefly on my knee as you excuse me. The touch waves through my gut and I hold my jaw clamped shut, looking down to where your woman's hand left its trace on the neurons in my knee. But it's not personal. It's not you – not yet.

I don't know how to make normal conversation anymore so I try to teach you how to count to five in one of the rural Filipino dialects I learned while I was away.

"*Usa, duha, tulo, upat, lima.*" I pronounce the numbers careful-ly. And I smile when I hear you repeating them with the French-Canadian accent you generalize to all non-English languages.

"Now you try it," I tell the pretty roommate. But she just waves her hands and laughs as if it's all impossible.

One of your brothers sticks his large fair head out of a door-way and waves you back into the hall. "Aunt Tammy won't let Janae throw her bouquet until you come back in," he says.

Somewhere in the divorce from Uncle Ned, Aunt Tammy decided to keep you. And now, the two of you have come here tonight with an agreement that you will stand beside her at the back of the mob of single, female wedding guests and keep the bridal bouquet from touching her in any way. Unlike Uncle Ned, Aunt Tammy is not a romantic. Even before all the trou-ble started between them, whenever she was asked what it was that brought her together with her husband she'd always just say, "Alphabetical order. Our gym teacher made us line up on the first row of the bleachers in the alphabetical order of our last names – and his came right after mine, obviously. That was it, kids. That was the magic."

After the wedding, back in the city where we go to university, I visit your apartment at least twice a week, sitting on the carpet, playing that nursing home card game the pretty roommate likes so well. You and I aren't alone together until that time I meet you unexpectedly roaming between the buildings on campus. You're laughing at me again when you find me standing in an alpine currant hedge outside the Student Union Building, eating the fruit right off the twigs.

"I thought those little red berries were poisonous," you say, plucking one yourself and frowning as you hold it up to your nose.

"That's the best thing about them," I explain. "Everyone thinks they're poisonous. That's why they're all still hanging here, uneaten and ripe and right in the open, left for people like us." I don't know why I say "us" – just some kind of cosmic slip, a stumble over the timeline, I guess.

I finally convince you to eat the currant you've picked, but there's nothing I can say to get you to try the fruit from the chokecherry tree limbs over our heads.

"Dude, that's ornamental fruit."

"Says who? It's perfectly good for food."

You laugh at me. "No, it isn't. I've eaten chokecherries before. It was a prank my brothers played on me. You can't tell me they don't taste like wet alum packed around a pit."

I scoff and toss a tiny, black cherry into my mouth.

"No way." You shake your head as I spit the pit into the bark mulch spread beneath the tree. "If you can eat ornamental chokecherries like that, either you've got extremely sophisticated taste or no sense of taste at all."

But you still walk away from the university with me that day. You climb the stairs to the scruffy, walk-up apartment I share with my matchmaker cousin and you look through every page of the photo album from my days in the Philippines.

"The dialects in the Philippines aren't even that hard to pick up. I learned to speak three of them while I was there." I'm just about bragging. "Here, I'll teach you to count to…"

"*Usa, duho, tuha…*" you interrupt in your French-Canadian accent.

It's a terrible moment. "I'm repeating myself…"

"Maybe a little. But it's okay. Anyway, it's all very interesting."

"Maybe the first time around." I roll my head and close the album. "Sorry."

You tell me it probably makes for better conversation than hashing over your adventures in the university's Womyn's Studies department. You pull the photo album out of my hands, flipping it open. "It's not exactly Home Ec.," you say. And now you're the one who might be boasting.

It sounds like a trap so I just shrug. "Are you – enjoying it?"

You slide your fingernail between two plastic pages that have been slicked together by the tropical humidity trapped inside the pockets of the album. "My classes are – lively, at times," you answer. And then you're talking, loud and fast, about the danged cleverness of the patriarchy – its expertness at keeping women distracted by details, missing key points, bickering with each other.

I wait until you're quiet again before I risk taking a long

sideways look at your face. Your neck is bent as you grimace close to a snapshot of a scorpion-like creature I'd found sunning itself on a village road early, early one morning. In my brain, I know you're not what I've been trained to believe is beautiful – nothing like the tawny, yielding sweetness of your pretty roommate. Your talk is fast and complicated but it all makes sense. And I know there's nothing to fear in it.

When you leave and I find one of your long, pale hairs caught in the threads of my sweater, I pull it free from my clothes. It moves in the air in front of me as I hold it between my thumb and my index finger. I wind it around the top joint of my finger, pulling it tightly enough to cut a white line into my flesh.

Even after all this, it takes weeks before I can admit that it's you and not the pretty roommate that keeps me coming to visit your apartment. My roommate-cousin is disgusted with me.

"I can see what you're doing, Brigham, even if you can't," he says. "You're getting lazy – and scared. Every pretty girl is a challenge, Dude. But you're balking at the challenge and settling for the sure thing."

It's an ignorant warning, and I try to take it as the gift he intends it to be. He doesn't even know you. I forgive him. And I keep coming back to you anyway.

We're high above the river, on the bridge. It's the only bridge in the city that's tall enough to guarantee an effective suicide. And it's the only bridge I've ever seen that's equipped with hundreds of metres of plumbing riveted to its flaky black girders. The city runs water through the pipes and turns the whole thing into a mechanical waterfall every July long weekend – like a bad sprinkler system watering nothing but the bridge's asphalt road and the river below. But tonight, it's Remembrance Day, and the pipes are dry and empty. This is where we are when you stop and rest your face in your hands, looking into the darkening east. Your elbows must be getting cold through your coat sleeves, bent against the steel railing beneath them.

"So tell me: if you were walking out here to jump to your death," you begin, "would you dive off the eastern side, or the western side?"

I smirk. "That's easy."

"Is it?"

"Yeah. I'd jump into the dark left behind by the sun – all poignant and miserable. That's usually what people are going for when they commit suicide. So, if I came here all distraught in the evening, like this, I'd definitely go over the eastern side." I curve my arm and arc it over the railing in a simulation of my swan dive. "But, if I stayed up all night and was coming here in the morning – which is more likely for me, I think – I'd go over the western side."

"Easy." You're nodding.

"I think about this stuff. Bridges are my thing," I say.

"Really?"

"Yeah, naturally. My name is Brigham. It means 'from the bridge town.'"

You laugh. "The bridge town? What's that supposed to mean? What kind of town doesn't have at least one bridge in it?"

I turn around and face the west. "A dry one, I guess. What can I say? That's what my name means."

"You know, I'm glad this came up," you say. "It is high time we talked about your name."

We each take a deep breath. You let yours out to ask, "How can you go through life being called 'Brigham' all the time?"

It's not the direction I thought we were headed. I blow out my own breath. "That's easy too. I've never been called anything else so I guess I can't imagine how much better life must be for the rest of you." I lean sideways, toward you, nudging you firmly enough to jostle your chin out of your hands.

You're standing up straight now, turning your back to the frozen pipes, facing the headlights on the bridge's busy roadway. "Fine, but – I mean, how come no one ever shortens your name?"

I shift to stand in front of you, a barrier between you and the traffic that doesn't see us. "Shorten it? Why? It's only two syllables long to begin with. And the H is silent and everything."

"Yeah, but they're such heavy syllables," you're arguing. "It's just weird that no one has a nickname for you, not even your cousin. It's not normal. You know what I mean?"

I lay my gloved hands on the railing, one on either side of you, not quite like an embrace. Something's been in our minds for weeks now but it's never been in our hands like it is right now. My face is almost directly over the crown of your head. You've got to be able to feel my breath on your scalp as I say, "Actually, no, I don't know what you mean."

You sigh as if you're frustrated with me. You're not looking up at me but you're talking and talking – still defensive because even as you stand between my arms, you're afraid this might not be what it seems. And, by now, that would be a catastrophe.

Your voice is transposed just slightly higher than usual as you say, "You see, Brigham, names don't really exist in the material world. They're just totally arbitrary social constructs.

Like, your parents gave you your name when you were a newborn baby because they wanted you to belong to them. And naming you was the most obvious way of emphasizing their connection to you, right? But then no one else ever renamed you with a nickname or anything and that's not normal."

I pull my head back so I can see you better. "Maybe it's just that my name doesn't lend itself to nicknames very well. Like, what would you even call someone with a 'heavy' name like mine? Briggy? The Hamster?"

You laugh, leaning forward until your forehead touches my chest. But you jerk back almost on contact. "Brigs!" you announce. "You could be known as Brigs. Wouldn't that look great stamped on the back of a football jersey?"

"A football jersey? Since when do you care about football jerseys?" I say, slipping up again, speaking as if I've known you far longer than I have.

"Whatever. Brigs – I love it. Starting now," you tap the end of my chin with your fingertip, "I am renaming you and calling you Brigs."

"As a totally arbitrary social construct," I lower my face toward you, so close my eyes can't focus anymore and I have to close them, "to show that I belong to you?"

You tilt your head and breathe the word, "Exactly," right into my mouth.

Later, when I learn to love you, I tell you so.

"I believe you," is what you say in return.

But when I tell you you're beautiful you call me a liar. You still do.

A little over ten months after Janae's wedding, I marry you.

You're twenty-one years old, and I'm twenty-two. Your university friends think it's madness and oppression, but I can tell you're thriving on all the indignation.

"A short engagement," you crow. "I think we've discovered a new, post-modern, Western relationship taboo. They all hate it. If I had French braids and a homemade calico dress they'd be able to understand it and denounce it. But as it is, there's nothing they can do but hate it."

And then you make me give you a high five.

The morning before our wedding, I accidentally press and twist on my razor blade against my skin and cut a long, horizontal gash into my throat. The cut is red and scabby enough for it to be the first thing you notice when I meet you on our wedding day. You laugh right at me and accuse me of trying to decapitate myself rather than marry you. I still don't think it's funny.

There's no groom's cake at our wedding reception. Maybe that's a shame. I know you keep your own little list of bridal regrets — the dearth of pictures, the way the printers used a "y" instead of an "i" in the spelling of my mother's name on the invitations. Then there was the way Dad kept circulating around the reception hall telling everyone what he paid for and precisely how much it cost.

"It's no one's fault but my own," you say, years and years later. "I couldn't hate myself more for caring about it. But I really, really did care."

I think what I remember best about the parts of our wedding day we spent in other people's company was that old man who shook our hands in the receiving line and thanked us for having the reception the same evening as the ceremony itself.

He said, "A wedding reception's nothing without a little sexual tension, eh kids?"

There was much more advice given than that. But if any of the guests knew to tell us that good husbands are like good anthropologists, none of them said so. An anthropologist: that's what you call me when you find me standing over your cluttered dresser top opening and closing some kind of contraption that's part scissors, part rubber stamp.

"Sheesh, Brigs, it's just an eyelash curler."

I hold it above my face so light glints off its metal before I turn and point the artefact toward you. "I don't think I've ever seen you use this."

"That's because I don't use it. Janae gave it to me ages ago when she was putting me through one of those beauty rehab sessions she calls makeovers."

I stand there, still pointing the instrument toward you.

You sigh like it's all very tiresome, but you do take the eyelash curler from me anyway. Leaning into the mirror, you pull your eyelids apart before pinching your upper lashes between the contraption's black bumpers. I don't get too close as I study the ritual with pretended nonchalance, silently measuring the movements of your reflection in the mirror. I watch, calculating, and mentally composing my ongoing thesis on a microculture that doesn't really belong to anyone but you.

My attention here means something to you, and you turn and step closer as you finish the curling manoeuvre, coming to stand beneath me, your arm curving around my waist. You wink your single curled eyelash at me, slowly, so I can see it all.

# Fourteen

We are back – back in the town where I'm not known as the kid with the highest grade point average in the graduating class of 1990. And I'm not known as the man who moved on to become one of the youngest-ever vice presidents of a major regional petroleum company either. Just like you said, I am indeed known here as "the one who found the body."

It hasn't been too difficult for us to stay out of town since Mom died here a couple years ago. But my cousin, Aunt Marla's daughter, is getting married this weekend. And the reception is going to be in the same church hall where people once straggled in to congratulate the newly married you and me. So here we are, back in town – the boys all fussy and hot in their wrinkly, white dress shirts, and you flicking glances over your shoulders like you're trying to catch someone looking at us with anything even vaguely like morbid pity.

We've arrived too early for the reception and, with all the people milling around, Aunt Marla's house is small and sweltering. That's why we're dragging our droopy boys down the street to a park Mom used to take them to. I ask the boys if they remember being here with her. They try but I'm not sure they remember anything at all – until they see the merry-go-round.

"Oh, *this* place," Scottie says.

The merry-go-round is one of those old, old ones installed in playgrounds the Lions Clubs and Rotarians built before you and I were born. I'm pretty sure most cities around here have banned them for safety reasons by now. But those kinds of hysterical cultural over-corrections take a long time to make it to little towns like this one. Maybe this merry-go-round was originally put here as part of some sort of attempt to recapitulate the 1960s space-flight training programs – like a beautiful token of hope in a generation of tiny, prospective astronauts. Who could have told the Rotarians we'd never really grow up to live in domed, glass space colonies full of classical music and bright white furniture?

The merry-go-round itself is a metal-clad disc with a radius equal to the height of our middle son – our Levi. The whole thing spins on a single, central pole that still glides freely, somehow, even though it's been standing out here in the wind and snow without being greased for thirty years. Out of the centre of the disc, steel bars spread out in rays. Each is flecked with a few remaining chips of primary-coloured paint. It doesn't make me happy to wonder how I can tell just by looking at them that these bars would taste like salt if I licked them – the panicky perspiration of the hundreds of desperate hands that have clung to them, braced against all the powers of centrifugal force.

Our boys are running ahead of us now, over the flat, un-irrigated grass to the playground. Maybe we would have been able to appreciate the dated equipment in a cool, retro sense if the imminent threat it posed to our kids wasn't quite so clear to us.

The sight of it all seems to have put space travel into your mind too. "Wow," you say, stopping at the edge of the park to lean back and cross your arms over your middle. "Look at this junk. It must be pre-Star Wars."

I shrug. "Probably. I know I can't remember the town without it."

"I'm tellin' ya," you're nodding. "Hey! Not so fast, you guys!"

And you're stomping over to the merry-go-round, catching it by one of the bars, pulling back with all your mass and strength to bring it to a stop. The boys lurch and stumble against the bars. "Let Benny get down," you say, as our sheepish older sons scoot their two-year-old brother to the edge of the disc. "What the heck were you guys thinking? This thing is actually really dangerous. Benny is too little to play anywhere near it. Okay?"

"Okay."

Scottie takes Benny's hand and helps him up the ladder of the slide instead. It's not safe either, but at least it operates under the more familiar and predictable perils of friction and gravity.

There's a wooden picnic table someone's pulled into the shade of a spruce tree in a far corner of the park, and you and I head there together to stay out of the sun. We sit on top of the table, turned to watch the kids play.

"So do we want to drive past it on our way out of town?" you ask me.

"Drive past it?"

"Yeah. The Mountain View Mobile Home Community."

I lie back on the tabletop, my arm bent beneath my head like a pillow, and I look up into the sky that's so blue it seems almost fake – like the blue screen that comes up on a television when there's no input. "Why would we want to drive past it?"

You're afraid you've upset me so you lie down beside me, resting your head on my elbow. "Just to see if her old trailer's still there. That's why they call them mobile homes, right? Because the whole thing could be gone by now. I hope it is."

The last time I asked Aunt Marla about it, she said the trailer Mom died in was still sitting vacant in the trailer park. Even after the way the landlord made us rush all Mom's stuff out of it before we'd finished burying her, he hadn't managed to rent the place to anyone else. But I hadn't heard anything more about the Dead Lady Trailer in years. Maybe you're right. Maybe it's gone – moved to another aluminum and fibreboard slum in some other little town where no one ever heard what happened to my mother.

But we won't be driving through the trailer park today. I know it as soon as I hear Benny start to wail. We've been distracted and looked away from the children too long and everyone is about to pay for it.

Scottie and Aaron are standing stunned at the bottom of the slide. Levi is still spinning around on the merry-go-round, by himself. But he's inching along the bar, moving toward the edge like he's trying to look for something fallen underneath it. We can all hear Benny crying but none of us can see him.

I'm running and – even though I know it won't do any good – yelling. "Where's the baby?"

Levi is so scared he can barely answer me. "Benny – fell off."

You've run to the merry-go-round from the other side so you're the first one to see Benny. From the neck down, his body has slid underneath the spinning disc. All you can see of him is his little blond head, awake but stunned, not crying anymore, lying with his face propped on one of his round, white cheeks in the sand. He's dusty and scared but he's safe where he is as long as he doesn't move. And then you see him pressing his palms against the ground, getting ready to rise.

"Stop, Benny! Head down!"

As we hear the sound of your voice, we understand it's inevitable. Everything's moving too quickly and too slowly – all at the same time. It means I don't quite reach the merry-go-round in time to haul it to a stop before the little boy hears you. And he has to look for you – he does it without thought. He jerks his head up like there's a line strung between the muscles in his neck and the vocal cords in your own. He lifts himself right into the orbit of the metal disc. It hits his scalp like the dulled edge of a buzz saw. All six of us scream at once.

I've stopped the spinning and now Levi is standing over Benny, struggling to undo it all by hefting his brother to his feet. Then he sees the blood. Both of Levi's hands come up to cover his mouth and nose and he turns away to gag.

"Scottie! Come and get Levi out of here!" you're calling.

Benny's angel-white hair is clumped into mucky red dreadlocks against the back of his head. The cut must be somewhere beneath it, gashed across the flesh over his occipital lobe. It must be the worst cut any of our kids has ever had.

"Ack – Brigs, did you see that?" you demand as you pull your cardigan off your shoulders and try to press the fabric to Benny's wound.

"What?"

"The blood comes spurting out the back of his head every time his heart beats."

There's no time for me to feel sick or sad or even to stop to get a good look at my baby's issue of blood. Benny is still fully conscious – even feisty. That will have to be enough for now. "Keep the sweater on it. Apply pressure," I say because that's what they always told us in Boy Scouts. It's all I can say before I order the rest of the kids into the minivan so we can get Benny to a hospital.

In the back of the van, Benny has stopped crying and he's fighting to keep your sweater away from his head. "You have to leave it on, baby," you're saying. But Benny keeps swatting and ducking, complaining and cursing in his broken toddler-English it's probably best we don't understand right now.

We drive right past the town's hospital – the one where I had my appendix removed when I was a kid. The building's been turned into a long-term care residence for seniors so we head out to highway. In ten minutes, we'll be at the hospital in the nearest town – the town where you lived while you were in high school.

"You can probably slow down a bit," you call from where you're holding onto Benny in the backseat. "It's just regular bleeding now. The horror movie's over. Right, Levi?"

Levi shudders behind the little hands he still holds pressed over his closed eyelids. He won't believe any of it.

I know I won't be able to see Benny's wound from the driver's seat but I glance at you in the rear view mirror anyway. You tell me later that the blood had been bright red and kind of thick – living blood oozing out of our baby's head like it was getting squeezed out of a tube, pulsing and pulsing. In the

141

back of the van, between all our boys, your hands and arms and clothes are covered in blood. And I remember a scene from a movie that used to make us laugh – the one where a character in bloody clothes turns to alarmed onlookers and says, "Oh, it's okay. This isn't my blood."

And this blood isn't yours either. All of our kids' blood is full of Rh antigens – those harmless little blood proteins that make your immune system freak out. You don't have them in your blood, but the boys inherited them from me. That's why you needed to get all those shots of immunoglobulin right in the butt every time you got pregnant. We needed to make sure your body didn't start trying to melt down our babies. But Benny's blood isn't my blood either. It's steeped with the B antigens you gave him – the ones that would make me sick if anyone tried to pipe your blood into me, no matter how much you might say you love me.

Benny is calm and even pleasant by the time we get to the hospital. "Do you still think we need to go in?" I ask.

You purse your lips and squint into Benny's head. "Uh – it's pretty flappy and oozy. We'd better have someone check it out."

We're the only people in the small town, weekend emergency room. You and Benny look dirtier and gorier than ever, now that you've been seated on a clean, white-sheeted gurney.

You hold the little boy against your body, I clamp his legs together so he can't kick, and a nurse with a warm, damp washcloth swabs Benny's scalp, looking to see the full extent of the cut. It isn't nearly as big as either of us expected – not quite two centimetres long – and it isn't bleeding at all anymore. The nurse comforts Benny with a gift of the most ludicrously over-dyed purple Popsicle I've ever seen. She leaves us, promising the doctor will be coming soon.

"I know," you say – which is a strange response. But you've already heard the doctor's voice through the curtains drawn around us. It wasn't his loud, authoritarian talk that gave him away. Within all the contrived officiousness of his voice is a sound you've known even longer than you've known me.

"It's Dan, isn't it?" you ask the nurse as she's trying to leave us.

She startles and starts to stammer. It's like she's trying not to answer, like she knows it's her duty to hide the secret first name of the doctor from all the bleeding riff-raff.

"Dan," you repeat. "Dan is the doctor here today, isn't he?"

"Uh, yeah," she admits.

When the nurse finally gets away, you breathe out an enormous sigh. "Brigs, Benny – you are about to meet Mummie's prom date."

I bend at the waist and laugh at you as you sit on the clean sheet, looking like an expendable extra from a slasher movie. We know this doctor – or, at least, you do. We are now at the mercy of one of your ex-boyfriends. Benny's been dying for a break in the tension and he laughs with me.

"Hey, that's Doctor Prom-Date, to you guys," you interrupt me through a little laugh of your own. There's still half of a smile on your mouth, and your eyes haven't quite finished their roll, when a thin but ordinary hand parts the curtain. And there he is in a white lab coat that fits him about as well as a Halloween costume: the boy you used to write letters to after you left that cousin of mine who wouldn't call you his girlfriend. That was years before you'd ever met me. They were long, handwritten letters like people used to write all the time – only the ones you sent to this boy usually had Joni Mitchell lyrics scrawled all over the outsides of their envelopes.

Here in the hospital, the stethoscope slung around his neck actually looks real. He's already read your name on the chart in his hands so there's no surprise left in his manner when we meet. You introduce me to him. We shake hands and everything, but we're both kind of stiff about it.

"It's not personal. He's like that with everyone," you'll tell me later. "And so are you, Brigs."

There are professional duties to be done, so the doctor starts trying to talk to our injured little boy. Benny knows not to trust him and sits stonily gripping his Popsicle while it melts into streams of indelible purple ink, dripping down his fist and onto your arm.

There's nothing at all left in either your or the doctor's voices to suggest what you must have meant to each other when you were both eighteen. He says, "That's no ordinary Popsicle. That's a special medical Popsicle. It cost the taxpayer about ten dollars."

You snort.

"No really, we have people eat them when they have chest injuries. If they start coughing up purple dye afterwards we know they're aspirating their fluids. It means they're in big trouble."

"Not like you, Benny."

"No, no. Not like Benny."

Benny's cut does need a stitch – but just one. Dr. Dan the prom date explains that we have a tricky parenting decision to make – one of those choices where no matter how we choose, everyone loses.

"If we try to anesthetise the area with a needle, it'll mean one more poke in the head – and it might not even work very well. Benny could end up feeling every bit of the stitching process anyway." If we'll agree, Dr. Dan will go ahead and sew up the breach in Benny's scalp without bothering to try to numb the skin first.

You sigh. "Okay then. Luckily for all of us, Benny here is one extremely tough little kid. Aren't you, Benny?"

The nurse wheels in a shiny steel tray full of equipment before the four of us – you, me, the doctor, and the nurse – start closing in on Benny. In your arms, he squirms and yells and throws his head back into your sternum, transferring a new smear of blood onto you and hurting his tender scalp. He's loud but so small there isn't room for all of us to grapple with him at once. I look at you over the top of his head.

"I've got this one, okay?"

You nod as you pass the little boy to me and step away. "I'll go check on the other kids."

The older boys are sitting mesmerized in a corner of the hospital foyer set up like a forest of fake rubber trees. They're slouched on chairs arranged around a television tuned to the all-cartoons-all-the-time station that we refuse to subscribe to on our TV at home.

Before the emergency room curtain drifts closed, you look back at Benny and the rest of us. You look back to see me and your prom date – me with my arms closed around Benny and your date bearing down on the child with a thin, curved needle like the one Nanny used to use for quilting. In the doctor's powdery, latex-gloved fingers, the needle is totally sterile, right up until it passes through Benny's hair. By the time we're all near enough to get the stitch into Benny's scalp, my own head is so close to the doctor's it would have been nothing for me to tip forward and kiss him, right on his face.

Benny yelps — once, twice — and drops the mushy medical Popsicle onto the clean floor. The stitch is in — blue nylon thread tied in a knot on the back of Benny's head. The nurse swoops up the Popsicle in a paper towel and pitches it in the trash right away, but it leaves a long purple stain on the white floor tiles anyway.

"I've got a few minutes before the ambulance gets here with a rogue diabetic who needs fluids and scolding," Dr. Dan says as we walk out of the empty emergency ward together. By now, I'm pretty sure he's a dork, like you and me. But he's a nice guy — nice enough for Benny to have already forgiven him and taken him by the hand as we go to find you and the rest of the boys. "Your boy's got his Mom's hair, hasn't he?"

"Yeah, they all do at this age. But they seem to outgrow it pretty quickly."

Dr. Dan hums. "She let me cut her hair once — at least, I'm almost sure that was her. It's a long time ago now, eh? That would have been during our first year at university. She'd run out of money and it ended up growing way out of control — nearly all the way down her back. But I was too freaked out to cut off any more than just a little bit."

I grin and kind of laugh — because there's nothing to say. And what is funny is that I know I'm not jealous of Dr. Dan, the prom date. I don't know how it's possible, but I know it's true.

"Not that it would have mattered much," he goes on. "Whatever hair I cut off has probably grown back a hundred times over since then. Right?"

"A thousand times over. Right."

I'm actually smiling when I look at him. He still has most of his hair but it's got a lot of grey in it. In a minute, you'll go ahead and tell him so – because you know that's the kind of awkward teenaged candour he'll still be expecting from you. And even then I won't be jealous. The prom, the scissors in your hair, all the letters, the fact that you already know what his hand would feel like if it were to touch you – none of it matters.

Maybe you're like Benny, who will always have a small scar on his scalp, underneath his thick blond hair, carved by the hand of Dr. Dan himself. In all this time, I still haven't lifted up every single hair on your head to examine all the skin underneath every one of them. Maybe if I did, I'd find that you have the same kind of scar. Only it wouldn't be all red and inflamed and puckered around a suture like Benny's is today. It would be smooth and flat and white – a little dead around the edges.

## Fifteen

I'm still finishing university when I learn to tell by the way the phone rings before eight o'clock in the morning that someone we know has had a dream that freaked them out.

It's happening again this morning, just as I'm closing the door behind me to leave for school. You wave goodbye to me as you plant our second-born son, baby Aaron, on your left hip and walk toward the telephone. The call will be a dream report from one of your girlfriends – or maybe Janae.

The dream could be anything.

"I'm at this barbecue, all normal and everything, but then I realize I've got a fiddler crab hidden inside my stomach. And I know if I move it's going to spaz out and slice me up."

It sounds weird but it's no mystery to you. The dream means the girl still hasn't come to terms with the miscarriage she had, years ago.

Then there are these ones:

"There's this shallow pond with a really thin layer of ice on its surface. And there's a big, red octopus lying at the bottom of it, like it's asleep or something."

148

And you know this girl needs a date.

That, you say, is how women usually dream – all in relationships and internal organs and fresh blood.

Men are different. We dream in phalluses. You say it's getting really, really boring – turning into the kind of thing any hack with one semester of undergraduate psychology or a copy of that *1001 Dreams Revealed* manual from the bookstore can unravel for himself.

Usually, all you have to say to the phallus dreamers is something like, "You're harpooning red octopuses? Really? Come on, dude, don't make me say it."

But you say what's really sick is how much men dream about money.

"I dream my Dad's dragged me out golfing with him. But I can't find the first tee so I have to start at the second one. So he's flipping out at me because we know there's no way we'll ever finish the round before it gets too dark."

So, someone's suspecting maybe he shouldn't have taken a whole decade to goof off before going back to school.

Sometimes, when the phone rings in the morning like this, it couldn't be any easier for you to show them what they're trying to tell themselves. All you have to do is repeat word-for-word what they just said to you.

"We're on this big hike through the jungle together, like a safari or something, and I'm carrying everything – "

"You're carrying everything."

"Yeah. Do you know what it means already? Because I'm not done –"

"YOU'RE CARRYING EVERYTHING."

149

"Oh."

But some people don't like it when girls like you – little student wives from the crummy walk-up apartments off Whyte Avenue – come storming into their dream worlds, kicking over all the cardboard set decorations. It's embarrassing. Your Dad knows it. He's become something like your dream interpreting agent – not that anyone would ever pay you for what you do. And maybe if you started accepting money to interpret dreams, you wouldn't be able to tell anyone anything anymore.

Anyways, your Dad gets all kinds of men to tell him their phallus-money dreams – the dude who works on his furnace, the other government guys at work, strangers on airplanes, it doesn't matter. Of course, he doesn't get them on the phone to talk to you themselves. Your squeaky white girl voice on the other end of the line, the sounds of our kids' cartoon videos playing on the TV in the background – that'd obliterate whatever mystique any of this might have. And, since you can't make money at it, your Dad is left with just the mystique to appreciate – that and being in on the secrets.

There are plenty of secrets here. When they tell you their dreams, they always tell you way too much – and it's dang awkward sometimes. The girl with the fiddler-crab-miscarriage dream? She told you about the dream over the dinner table at your parents' house.

"Did you hear that, Brigs?" you demanded in the car on the way home. "What was I supposed to say to her?"

I squinted down the road, trying to remember exactly what she'd said. "Tell me again."

When you repeat the dream yourself, I can tell what it

means too. There's something about hearing it told in your language and voice that makes it perfectly clear to me.

"So if you didn't call her on the miscarriage, what did you end up saying to her?"

You throw your hands up. "Well, I panicked and just made up something stupid and generic about body image before I got the heck out of there."

The dreams always tell the truth. But sometimes you need to lie – and I'm always glad when you do. "You shouldn't tell people you can interpret dreams unless they're going to stay strangers to us forever," I'll say as we slink out of another nearly ruined dinner party where you stopped just short of telling someone her dream about running a struggling roadside produce stand actually means she doesn't trust her husband anymore.

"I know, I know."

Maybe your Dad's way of handling the dream interpretation business is smarter. When your Dad's got a big dream from a big man that needs interpreting, he'll have them type it out in an email and then he forwards the whole thing to our address. You'll tease it out, fire it back, and wait – always so smugly – to get the reply about how you were right on. It's funny – when the big men write back to your Dad about what you've told them, they always refer to you, the unknown interpreter, as "he." And the last thing your Dad would ever do is correct them. I guess he figures it shouldn't matter to us if the phallus-money-dreamers are happier picturing you all skinny and shorn and flat, sitting in a lotus position on top of a mountain somewhere.

As far as your Dad is concerned, the highlight of your dream interpreter career came when you analyzed that dream his boss had about losing all his teeth. Your first reply in the email thread was just one line: "Ask him how long it's been since his braces came off."

That blew their minds. You knew it would. You did it on purpose because showmanship is important in an endeavor like this one. It doesn't actually matter to you when his braces were removed. But it seems like all orthodontia survivors have nightmares about their teeth – even you. You'll be deep in it, dreaming you're bent over a stainless steel sink, spitting out blood and saliva and pretty white teeth. When the psychic parachute finally opens, you wake up, feeling around inside your mouth with your tongue, so relieved you could cry. If anyone knows what the tooth dreams mean, it's you. They're about dreading the inevitability of other people finding out what you really are – finding out you're a sham.

It's time for you to pick up that ringing, early morning phone. It is Janae – just like I said it would be.

"Okay, so I dreamed there's this ghost in my house. First it takes over my cat, then my oven, then my computer."

You're laughing.

"It's not funny. It was a ghost and it was wrecking everything. It was scary."

"Sorry, Janae. But – well –congratulations. You're starting to be ready to get pregnant again."

"Yuck."

"I didn't say you were happy about it – just preparing for it. It's okay. Go ahead."

"Do you really think I am?"

You sigh loudly enough for her to hear you through the

phone. "This has got nothing to do with what I think. It never does. I'm only telling you what *you* think."

The phone call veers off somewhere else and doesn't end until about an hour after I've left the apartment. Scottie has finished eating breakfast but you leave the milky cereal bowls on the table and lie down in bed again. It's been another rough night, bouncing the bad baby in the dark.

Your head touches the pillow and it all comes back to you. There's something in the smell and feel of your own side of the bed that resurrects the dream you were having, just hours ago. It's another variation on an old theme – not quite a tooth dream, but close. It's the one you say you hate more than any other dream in your entire repertoire.

Your dream is not clever or artistic or mysterious or – anything. It's just literal and lame and – if you ask me – as unlikely as heck. It's just me, leaving you.

"Stop dreaming that," I say, shaking you back and forth where you lie on your back in our bed, later that night. I won't stop shaking until you start to laugh at me. "What have I ever done," I say as I climb on top of you, "to make you think I'm going to leave you? Aren't I nice to you?"

"Yes."

"And good to the babies?"

"Yes. But it's not like I can help what I dream, Brigs."

"No?"

"No – and you can't help what I dream either." We look at each other, quiet for a moment, just inches away from each other's faces. "Hey Brigs, if you weigh almost twice what I do, how come I'm not squished flat every time you lie on top of me?"

I smirk. "Because when I'm on top of you I'm always supporting most of my own weight with my arms and legs."

"What? No, you're not."

"Sure I am."

"Show me," you say.

I shake my head. "I'm actually really heavy. You won't like it."

"It doesn't matter if I like it. You have to show me. It bothers me to think I might not really know how heavy you are. I mean, what if you were to drop dead someday, right on top of me?"

I laugh. "That could definitely happen."

"Right. And I need to know I can escape – if it ever does happen."

I sigh and all your hair blows back against the pillow. "Alright then. Are you ready?"

You nod, and I feel you tense your muscles underneath me, bracing yourself. And that's when I collapse, every ounce of my body from the neck down crushing down onto yours.

Your eyes get wide and your breath hisses out as your ribs compact beneath me. "Brigs," you gasp with an extra-long S.

"See what I mean?"

You cough. "Yeah. Okay. Get off me."

I don't move at all. "But I'm dead, remember? You have to figure out how to escape without my help."

You start to struggle, pulling your arms free, pushing my shoulders away. It jostles me from side to side but the bulk of me stays right where I dropped it in the first place. "Dude, I can't even scream," you rasp.

"Yeah?" I let myself settle even further, resting my forehead against the pillow, beside your head. "This was a great idea.

Imagine if we hadn't practiced this before it really became an emergency."

You try to thrash yourself free. It lasts until you pant out a little laugh and drop your arms so your palms are upturned in a surrender pose. "You're too heavy. I can't get away."

"Sure you can." I say it languidly. "You have to. I'm still dead."

Your breath is getting fast and shallow. "Brigs – I'm going to have a panic attack. I'm not kidding."

"Yes, you are. Come on. Use your legs. They're way stronger than your arms."

You're panting and making weak little Kung Fu sounds underneath me. I don't admit out loud that it's all very enjoyable. I don't have to admit it.

"Hey," you snap, "knock it off. This is not sexual."

I laugh. "Sure it is. It always is."

"No. It isn't." You're trying to be stern.

"Come on," I drawl, "you've got to get away. How are you ever going to manage to mutilate my dead hand and cut a bone out of it the way you've always wanted to if you're trapped underneath me until the end of time?"

"Ha!" you yell as you throw one of your legs free.

"There ya go," I cheer. "Now all you have to do is roll away from me."

You're twisting and writhing. "I can't."

"That's right," I say, still deadweight on top of you. "You can't get away."

Underneath me, you're popping P sounds. "P-patriarchal violence."

I shake my forehead against the pillow. "Nope. It's not me.

It's got nothing to do with my own force. It's just gravity. You know – the earth and space and everything. All of nature pulls me down right here."

"I can't."

"Neither can I. You and I – this is not something we can ever get out of. Okay? Do you believe me yet?"

Your only answer is to start fighting again. Your effort is stronger but its effects are weaker as your muscles burn off their oxygen – the air your lungs can't expand to replace anymore.

"Now," I say, moving toward the ending. "Will you please stop dreaming that I'm trying to leave you?"

You still don't say anything. But you stomp your free foot into the mattress, yelling as best you can without any breath. You rock back and forth until you create enough momentum to pry yourself out from underneath me. All free and triumphant, you sit up, laughing, panting, smacking me on the back with one hand.

"I'm out," you say. "I broke the gravity. How do you like *that*?"

And the truth is I like it just fine. I'll never tell you, but I cheated. The truth is I used my own muscles to help rock myself away from you in the end. I let you out. The truth is nothing is broken.

## Sixteen

The conduit is opening again. It happens through the phone, as it often does. This time, the caller is your Dad. And he's mad — so mad he's quiet and speaking almost a full octave below his usual pitch.

"I can't trust myself to deal with it like a civilized person," he's telling you. "I need you to take it from here."

"Dad thinks I'm civilized?" you ask me after you've hung up.

And I almost laugh. Your powers of civility are not what have moved your father to call you. He's not looking for decorum. He's looking for justice. I can imagine him right now — still sitting on the edge of his bed with the phone in his hand, thinking about how he'd made a mistake when he failed to name you Wormwood.

It makes me laugh because it's funny — the way the family wants you to stand up at their funerals when they're sad and say something to tilt the hurt until they can feel it just right, in a way they can manage. But when they're angry, the same people you comfort want you to stand up and say something awful — something to rattle a load of brimstone out of the sky.

That's what your Dad is calling for today. He wants brimstone. He wants it yellow-green and stinking and burning and falling all over the crummy municipal cemetery where his parents are buried under sandy gravel and a skiff of grass that never quite gets green. It's a cemetery set into the side of a hill with a view of the Rocky Mountains on one side and a custom cattle feedlot on the other – cows and flies and manure as deep as muskeg. The feedlot cemetery – it's not Butcher Hill. It's the graveyard for the dead on the other side of your family.

"I can't believe it," you're telling me now. "I cannot believe something this ridiculous is actually happening."

I listen as you explain how your uncles went to visit your Granddad's grave on Father's Day – just a few days ago – and discovered the headstone that had been sitting there, waiting for the end of the world, marking their father's grave for the last twenty-one years, was gone.

"Unbe-frickin'-lievable," you say as you're looking up the number for the offices of the town that manages the Feedlot Cemetery.

The missing headstone was one of those slabs the government will award to veterans, if they ask. I don't remember seeing it myself, but you tell me it was grey granite cut into a rectangle, flecked with starry black and marked with your grandfather's name and his rank in the Canadian Armed Forces.

"Warrant officer," your Dad has told us. "That means he earned it – in Sicily. Normandy wasn't the only beach."

And now the headstone is gone.

Before they got too mad to deal with it, your Dad and uncles found out a cemetery groundskeeper had moved their father's stone. The almighty man with the mower said he couldn't take it anymore – that tiny space between your grandparents' headstones that made it too hard to maneuver his machinery, or whatever. So he took one of the headstones out – the smaller one, the one we got for free through a government program, the soldier's stone.

"They claim they've still got it, and it's safe and sound in a shed somewhere." And that's all your Dad can tell us before he knows he can't say another word about it.

You've punched your way through the touch-tone menus and connected with the town hall. I can hear you speaking into the telephone. Your sentences are short and hard.

"I need to talk to the town manager – Right now – No – I understand – No, I don't need the cemetery bylaws explained to me. I need my grandfather's headstone back. I need someone to show a dead veteran some respect – Listen – You have got until two o'clock tomorrow afternoon to send me a photo of the headstone. Two o'clock – Write it down. I need proof that someone knows exactly where the headstone is and that it's undamaged – If I don't see the picture in my email inbox, I'm calling the police – I'm going to tell them the truth. I'm going to tell them the headstone has been stolen. And I'm going to send the police looking for you."

It doesn't end there. You're on the computer for the rest of the night, writing a press release, sending it out to newspapers, pasting it up on the baffling stonewall the town administration has thrust up to protect the petty despot who cuts the grass and rearranges the monuments at the Feedlot Cemetery.

"He must be the mayor's troubled nephew or something,"

you say into the computer screen. "They're all inbred and nepotistic down there. And you know what we are to them, Brigs – a family like us? We are nobodies."

I squirm the way I always do when you get like this.

"Well," you're still saying as we lie in bed that night, "they've messed with the wrong family of obscure little nobodies this time."

Your press release is picked up by the daily newspaper in the city closest to the Feedlot Cemetery. They devote most of a page to the story, complete with a photo you sent of your grandfather standing by a fountain in Italy in the 1940s.

Across the country, back in Halifax, the story runs in the newspaper your grandfather used to deliver when he was a kid. Its tone is cautionary – a warning about moving out west and vanishing into oblivion.

The newspapers all quote the sound-bite you've crafted for them. "My grandfather fought the Fascists for us, so the least we can do is fight city hall for him."

It works. There's a town councillor and then the mayor on the phone apologizing and telling you how disgusted they are and promising this never would have happened if they hadn't been away on summer holidays.

"So do you want us to have the groundskeeper re-install the marker? We'll make him waive the fifty dollar fee and do it for nothing."

"No," you say. "We're coming to do it ourselves. You can tell the groundskeeper he'll never touch that headstone with his bare hands ever again."

Plans are made for me and you and your Dad to go to the

Feedlot Cemetery to put the stone back on the grave. Of course, you're pleased about how it's worked out. I don't mind that. What bothers me is the way you glory in this – I'm not even sure what it is. We've come calling for justice but maybe this is more than just a settled score. Maybe it's vengeance. I'm never sorry you don't really have wings, but sometimes I'm gladder than ever – like now, when the wings on your back might not be downy and henhouse benign but hard and hooked like a bat's.

I am here with you anyway, in the sun and the high August heat, stomping the sole of my boot against the back of a shovel, cutting into the upper layer of the cemetery turf like the most brazen, daylight grave-robber ever. The real grave-robber – the one you foiled – the Feedlot Cemetery groundskeeper, is leaning against a backhoe at the entrance of the graveyard, working hard at not watching us. You're in the back of our pickup truck with a square-nosed shovel, pushing a load of gravel toward the tailgate so you can rain it down into the trough I've dug for your grandfather's stone.

Your Dad levels the gravel and tamps it down – slowly, sadly. If the gravel bed is uneven, the stone might strain and crack over time. And there'd be no one to blame for it – no one to accuse in the press release – no one but ourselves.

When it's ready, it takes all three of us to lift the granite marker into place. We set it at the foot instead of the head of your grandfather's grave – in a place flanked with swaths of grass wide enough for anyone to turn a mower without any complaints. The stone is much heavier than we expect it to be, but we manage it anyway.

We're all sitting on the ground, panting and sweating, when

*Jennifer Quist*

it's over. The air is blowing down the cemetery hill like the blast from a hair dryer, stirring up the smell of manure and hay from the feedlot.

"Hot," you say. And you're bending, lower and lower, bowing until your cheek rests against the smooth, granite plane of the headstone itself. The granite beneath your cheek draws the heat from your flesh, diffusing it outward, away from you, across the stone's hard surface. The serif etched at the top of the W in "Warrant Officer" looks like it's about as long as the top of your thumbnail is wide, so you slide the end of your nail into it. It fits perfectly.

I hear you hum, like you're happy – or at least satisfied. "It's nice down here, Daddy," you say. "It's cool."

Your Dad isn't looking at you. It's been too much and he's had to pull away again.

But I'm still here. And I rest my hand on the stone, beside your face. Even in the sun, the rock is cold against my palm. Just like you, I feel something leaving me – something hot and dangerous we need to abandon here if we're ever going to be right again.

You're still on your knees with your face on the rock. But you've moved the nail of your thumb to the letter C, tracing its arc back and forth in the groove cut near the centre of a long Scottish name. It's your grandfather's name, your father's name, your name – the one you used to call yourself before you took mine.

"Feel it for yourself, Dad. It's smooth and cold and it's good."

Your Dad is turning to look at you. He doesn't quite smile. "Come on," he says. "Get off it. Move out of the way so I can

162

take a picture of it for your uncles. We need proof that it's safe."

You're slow to leave the stone. "Isn't it weird?" you begin. "It's so weird. Somewhere, in the earth there's a big, cold, billion-year-old rock like this already waiting for everyone."

"Come on." Your father jostles you, holding out his hand, his palm pressed right into the hollow between your shoulder blades – the flat, empty expanse of your back.

# Seventeen

It's you who takes the RSVP card out of the wedding invitation envelope and mails it back marked yes. You do it even though I tell and tell you I don't want to go.

There's no arguing with you. "Forget it, dude. Deirdre is finally getting married to a man of her own. It looks like she's given up on you. It's got to be tough for you, but we need to make an effort to celebrate with her anyway."

You make me crazy sometimes.

I never should have told you about Deirdre – the woman from my class in university who once looked at me across a table as messy as an unmade bed, strewn with notes for the group project we were working on. She sighed and hauled out that hackneyed old line – the one that goes, "How come all the good ones are married?"

"She is just a colleague," I tell you – again. It's true – for me, anyways. It's still true even though Deirdre has gone from studying at the same school as me to working for the same big petroleum company as me.

You ignore my protest – my honest statement of a fact.

When it comes to Deirdre, you always do. "I don't get this girl," you say. "Every engineering school in the whole world is jammed full of men. She should have had her pick. Why did it have to be you?"

"It's not me." I'm loud and petulant. "It's this guy – this Mitch guy."

You purse your lips and hum. "I wonder if Mitch knows about you."

You're enjoying it. It's clear. And it's not just because, all this time, Deirdre has been paying you a dazzling kind of compliment. She affirms our life together far more than she's ever threatened it.

"Of course he knows about me. Mitch works for us too," I hurry. "He's an engineer in the Edmonton office where Deirdre works. He knows me. And I'm sure he never bothers to think about me – ever."

You hum. "Is he tall?"

I shrug. "Tall-ish."

"Taller than Deirdre?"

Just when I thought we were moving on to Mitch, Deirdre's future, I see you're winding the discussion back toward me after all. You want to know if Mitch is a good match for Deirdre – a better one than me. The truth is the woman looks like she could be a sister to me. She's tall and strong and pale and loud, like the lead soprano in an opera by Wagner. I do understand that Deirdre and I look good together. Why did they have to take that picture – the one from the competition where Deirdre and I were sent to represent the university? The school flew us all the way out to Halifax and made sure we were photographed at the awards ceremony – me in a cheap charcoal-coloured suit and Deirdre in red lipstick and a black cocktail dress. The photo ran in the newspaper back in Edmonton. You came home with three copies of it piled into the basket on the bottom of the baby stroller.

"This is so totally going in our scrapbook," you cackled over the scissors as you clipped the photos out of the newspapers.

Good together – I hate to hear you say it, you and the lady at the coat check in the Halifax banquet hall who handed me Deirdre's long red dress coat saying, "I went ahead and got your wife's too while I was back there."

I've never confessed what the coat-check lady said – not to you. But Deirdre heard it.

I try to picture Mitch, Mr. Deirdre, in my mind – nondescript, plain old Mitch from the Edmonton research and development office. I want to see him in charcoal grey with a Valkyrie on his arm.

"I think he's about her height," I tell you.

"But you're not sure?"

"Not really."

"Then we definitely need to go to this wedding."

It isn't easy to do. Deirdre gets married while we're still living up north. We drive for five hours through November ice and salt to make it to the city – to the old Protestant cathedral that will look pretty in Deirdre and Mitch's wedding pictures.

The ceremony has just barely begun as we come in late and sit in the back. Deirdre is already at the front of the church. Through her veil, we can see her broad back and her long white neck.

"Look," I whisper. "I told you they're the same height."

The wedding itself is short and political. The officiator is actually a government cabinet minister, and he can't help but slip the name of the Premier into his remarks.

When he's finished, Mitch and Deirdre turn around to face the rest of us. They're arm in arm, pacing away from the altar. They're halfway up the aisle – a march blaring on the cathedral organ – when Deirdre stops, just for an instant. She's seen me – seen my own broad, pale face looking back at hers from the last row of the chapel. She raises the hand that isn't threaded through Mitch's arm and waves. Everyone else turns to see me. And I feel a little sick.

Your elbow stabs into my side. "Go ahead, Brigs. Wave back at her."

I nod – once for Deirdre and once for Mitch.

When the organ stops, I can hear you laughing – everyone can. "Did you see that?"

I hustle you out the chapel door – the other chapel door, the one Deirdre didn't use. But all the doors lead to the same foyer, the one where Deirdre and Mitch are lined up between their wedding attendants, waiting to be congratulated on their life together.

When it's our turn to greet them, you shake Deirdre's hand with both of yours and she claims she doesn't remember the time, years ago, when she met you in person once before. I cringe as she says it, but the whole story just seems to make you love her even more. You still haven't quite stepped aside before Deirdre starts to move. She's hugging me. There's a bouquet of calla lilies and ribbons pressed against my shoulder blade. I feel the heat rising from the white satin pinched beneath her arms.

And I'm sick all over again.

We're out in the street, walking back through the dark city blocks towards our car. You stop laughing long enough to rise up on your tip-toes, holding out your arms like a mummy, lowering the pitch of your voice, making yourself as much like Deirdre as you can. "Oh Brigs, you came," you quote in nothing like Deirdre's voice. "I can't tell you how much it means to me that you came all this way."

I can't stand it. I snatch you off your feet, my arms closed around your torso, and I spin you once and then again, in circles on the slippery sidewalk. Your legs fly out straight behind you, your feet barely missing the parking meters, and you start to squeal, but the spinning takes your voice away. You've buried your face in the wool of my coat, against my shoulder.

"Stop," I say as we turn. "Stop it."

I'm setting you down, your feet on the top of a retaining wall that runs along the sidewalk, beneath the wedding church. The extra height of the wall brings your face close enough for me to look right into your eyes.

"Stop." I say it again. I say it even though I know you're not jealous.

You're laughing, kissing my cheeks and my forehead, your hands on my face. "Sweet, sweet Deirdre," you say. "My favourite rival – one weak and meaningless, just another human being – one you can halt in the middle of her own wedding march."

"You do not have any rivals."

"Oh, that's not it," you interrupt. "That's not it at all."

You're reaching for my hand, making that mark again, drawing the line along the bone from my knuckle to my wrist.

"I do have a rival. And it will never get old or fat or married. Heck, Brigs, it could be here with us right now, for all we know."

It's this again. "Don't say it – "

"I will say it." You push at my chest, stepping down from the wall, walking backwards along the sidewalk, calling to me. "My one true rival – it's coming for you whether I dare to say it or not."

# Eighteen

You're laid out under the lights, your head held in a brace, mouth wide open. The man in the mask and goggles is leaning over your face, his nose hidden but just inches from yours. Behind the safety lenses, his eyes are wide and alert – not a trace of social recognition in them. This deadened human closeness – it must be what we mean when we call things "clinical."

There's a bitter taste of bleach at the back of your mouth where your tongue sprouts out of the walls of your throat. And there's a sound, deep inside your head, travelling into your brain through the Eustachian tubes that connect your pharynx to your ear canals. The sound is a scrape, scrape, scraping that goes on and on somewhere within your jaw.

"So now we're using our tiny little files here to grind out what the drills couldn't get at. Would you like to see what the files look like?" he has asked you.

"No, I'm good," you've answered, all in vowels around the rubber dam clipped to your numbed gums.

He had paused before he clamped the dam on you. He'd flicked a glance at his assistant. "See if we still have the paediatric-sized one."

It's one of our secrets – that inside your head is a mouth like a child's. And I always hate it when anyone else finds out – even people like him.

You rolled your eyes at me when you realized it. "Professional dental care is not intimate." That's what you told me. But how can it not be? The warmth, the pink, moisture, the smell – not even our kids know you that well anymore.

In the dentist's chair, they've left the lead-lined X-ray apron draped over your shoulders and chest, all the way down to the tops of your legs. They tell you it's for convenience, because they have to keep taking X-rays – making sure they've obliterated every last cell out the canals in the roots in that one, evil tooth of yours. But lying underneath the apron, you suspect the hot heaviness of it is actually there to treat your low-grade shock. It's coming and going in sickening, suffocating waves. The apron makes you think of one of those heated blankets you've only seen a few times before – the ones taken from special cupboards in the backs of emergency wards or out of ambulances at the scenes of car crashes.

It's not a standard dental cavity gone amok that's brought on this root canal. In fact, today is the first time you've ever had a tooth filled at all – the first time you've heard a dental drill working anywhere near your mouth. It's strange, but you're going from having completely virginal teeth to having a full-on root canal in one afternoon.

Somehow, your teeth just never succumbed to cavities – not even when you were a kid, not even when you had a full set of braces. Your teeth still don't get cavities, though you only floss on the weekends. Like a real Holy Incorrupt Saint, your mouth simply does not decay. Against all time and nature, your teeth are glistening, white, and beatified.

Even if your teeth don't rot – not like mine – it turns out they're still susceptible to rare degenerative conditions. The dentist says one of the bicuspids in your upper jaw – one that looks completely pristine from the outside – is actually in the middle of a slow, inexplicable fit of suicide.

"Internal resorption," the dentist called it. He actually sounded a bit excited when he picked it out of your X-ray during your routine check-up. "It's one of those ironic diseases. We're all supposed to love irony nowadays, aren't we?"

You wouldn't fake a smile for him – not about this.

"You see," he explained, "the tooth thinks it's trying to repair itself from some kind of internal stress – a bit like a broken bone."

"I didn't know teeth could do that."

He nodded. "That's right. They can't. But this one is trying its darnedest. Unfortunately, the cells it sends to fix things end up taking the tooth apart. It's like they get stalled in the demolition phase and never make it to the repair phase – since, for teeth, there is no such thing as a repair phase, really. It's strange, all right – and rare. But it's not cancer," he added, not quite out of nowhere.

It left us startled, wondering how we got to be talking about cancer at all. The dentist really didn't know that much more about your tooth disease himself. The best he could do was to send you home with a brand new article photocopied out of *The Western Journal of Dental Sciences*.

That was our regular dentist – the one who seems to be away on scuba diving vacations for half the year. This new dentist, the one leaning over you now, is a specialist. From behind his mask, he asks permission to show your X-rays to his colleagues. And for a few days, you and your rare tooth disease will be hot stuff in the local dental community.

Across town from the endodontist's clinic, in my office, I'm sitting in front of a computer screen, worrying about your appointment. I made my mark working in a northern boomtown when the kids were just babies, and my company rewarded me with a junior vice president position here in a city on the plains.

No matter what you say, I do think about you while I'm at work when you're not actually within my field of vision. I've left my cell phone on my desk beside my keyboard just in case you need to call me from the dental clinic again. I keep picking it up to make sure it's still on.

"Brigs," you said when you first called me from where you were hiding in the stairwell outside the posh misery of the endodontist's office. "I think I might leave. I don't think this is unfolding the way it's supposed to."

"Did they start yet?"

"No. I haven't seen any sign of the Great and Powerful Oz. But his receptionist is trying to get me to sign this form saying I've been properly informed about a whole bunch of stuff no one has ever informed me about."

I stand up. "Well, don't leave yet. Go back inside, get them to explain everything, and hang in there. It's okay."

The empty air on your end of the phone is hollow and funny. You're still in the stairwell, trying not to cry, and I can tell you hate yourself.

"Aw, it's okay," I say. "In two hours, it will be all over."

173

And then I can tell you're hating both of us.

I try something else. "Come on. Remember when Aaron cracked his back tooth wrestling with Scottie? And he was too little to tell us there was anything wrong until it was all abscessed and dangerous?"

You sniff. "I know, I know."

Aaron's accident was years ago now, when he was just a toddler. We had to take him to a paediatric dental specialist – a dentist who could drug kids to sleep before treating them. The dentist wasn't in the room yet when the anaesthesia team gathered to press that tiny black gas mask over Aaron's nose and mouth. Flat on his back on the table, the boy was frantic – like he was fighting for his life. He was sure he was being killed. It didn't matter that you were standing right there telling him not to struggle and not to be scared. He thought he was dying even though it was you who held his shoulders down and looked into his eyes while the doctors turned on the gas. And when his body went limp, you didn't believe the anaesthetist when she told you Aaron was already asleep. How could he be sleeping when he was still making that noise after you let go of his shoulders – a high, repeating, rattling alarm sounding through his open mouth? She called it a "little hiccup" – said it happened all the time. And then, while someone threaded a tube down his throat behind her, she smiled at you and showed you the door. Once you'd finished betraying your son, you were just in their way.

"Your tooth is in serious trouble. And the problem's not going to just go away on its own, right?" my voice says over your phone in the stairwell of the endodontist's office building. "You don't want to lose it – not when you're awake, not in real life."

174

"I know. I know."

"So go."

You promise you'll turn off your phone and head back inside the waiting room. The receptionist tries not to look smug as you hand her the waiver forms, dated and signed.

I'm on my feet at the sight of you coming through the door of my office. You've come all the way up to the top floor of the glum, brutalist building where I go to work every day. You've been hoisted up in the elevator, you've come through the glass doors of the office and smiled at my secretary with the half of your face you have the power to move, and you've made your way down the hallway to find me. Now you're sliding your arms inside my suit jacket and closing them around my ribcage. I'm crushing your face into my chest with one hand and pushing the door closed the other.

"Are you okay?" It's as stupid a question as it ever is, but I ask it anyway – just like we all do.

You turn your face, resting your cheek against me so your mouth is free and you can speak – lopsided and woolly. "I went in there and lay still while he hollowed out my living tissue and packed me full of plastic and silver. I just lay there like a cadaver for hours and let him do it. And near the end – I started slipping. My brainstem got all slow and sick, and I had to consciously tell myself, 'breathe and breathe and breathe,' every single second."

I run my tongue over the ceramic crown anchored in my own mouth. "Yeah, it's always kind of an awful procedure."

Your hands are on my forearms, your elbows straightening, forcing a distance between us. "Brigs – he was embalming me.

175

They just did one tooth this time but I know eventually it will all be finished. He was trying to get the dead off me so I could be presentable among the living again. *Embalming me.* I never wanted that. I'm meant for burning, not for emptying out and keeping."

There's nothing to do but laugh. I do it quietly and carefully and — mostly importantly of all — kindly. "Hey, don't think about it that way," I say. I'm sitting down, bending into my big vice president's chair that still feels to me like a prop in a play I'm acting out. I'm pulling you with me, onto my lap. No matter what you've just been through today, your body feels like it always does to me — like it's supposed to feel. "Cadaver," I scoff. "But you're all warm and soft. You're not dead. Though you might still be in shock — and a little bit silly, maybe."

You sit across my thighs, shoulders rounded, staring out the window at the dirty, concrete parking garage across the street. I glance at the closed door and think about sliding a hand inside your clothes. But this isn't that kind of play. And I know it's best just to keep still and wait. When you finally move again, it's to wipe at the numbed corner of your mouth. You look surprised when your fingers come away dry — no blood, no spit, no fluid of any kind.

And I can see the light returning as you shrug. "Silly — maybe. But Brigs," you look into my face, still faintly sad, "what if my head really did fill up with cancer? I mean, don't you ever worry about losing me?"

I sit back. And I know I don't worry about losing you — ever. I don't know why. Maybe I've seen you wrestle your own death too many times — there in those hospital delivery rooms when the tiny blood vessels burst in your face and you lose the power to speak and the portal to the world outside this one opens through your flesh – but then you just live on through it. Or maybe that's not it at all. I don't know. But I can tell – I can tell just from your pressure and warmth against me, across my legs, against my shoulder – that I won't ever live one moment here without you.

# Nineteen

The year I graduate from university is the year we move house together for the first time, right out of the capital city. There's nowhere for us to go but north, to the oil sands mines. It's the only way to pay back all the money we borrowed to finish the nine years of university we have between the two of us. And the only way to get to the oil sands by land is on Route 63 – that one, jammed, two-lane highway through the wilderness. So we're careening through the boreal forest right along with the logging trucks and the industrial wide-load trailers and the Mustangs that run on booze and testosterone. Through their windshields, the men see the silhouette of your long hair in the driver's seat of our car. They come up fast, staring at you through the glass – in spite of me and the kids in their car seats and the fact that you're pregnant with Levi, our third son. The men are leering sideways as they cross over the solid yellow centre line to pass us. Maybe you'll get used to it over the next few years, but I never will.

The sight of farmland ended hours ago. It was encroached upon by the forest until the sprawling ranches shrunk to nothing more than a few small herds of red cattle foraging between the aspen trees.

"No more pastures," I announce – quietly.

In the backseat of our small, economy car, the kids are starting to get restless in their five-point harnesses – pinned down by mazes of nylon straps and plastic clips at their shoulders and hips like little chimpanzee astronauts. It's too bad that when they're awake, they don't have any of that sad, stoic astro-chimp sense of resignation. Before we left the capital city, some of your grittier friends suggested you drug the boys with an over-the-counter anti-nauseant so they'd sleep through most of the trip.

"Nah. If they're anything like me," you said, "pills won't settle them down." The boys are sleeping now, but not because you drugged them – I'm pretty sure.

We're still an hour south of the Fort McMurray town-site when the road climbs, rising out of the green trees and into the old, burnt forest. Back when we were kids, a colossal forest fire ate up hundreds of hectares of the land south of the city. The crest of this hill is where the flames burned right up to the gravel shoulders of the highway, climbed to the tops of the tall, thin trees, bending them over the asphalt in a hellish, orange-red arch, clawing out for the fuel of the treetops on the other side of the road. The policemen stood in the middle of the highway, behind their barricades, with the bulldozers and the teenaged forest-firefighters who rubbed at their eyes and leaned against their shovels. And they all just watched it go.

When it was over, nothing came after the fire to finish off what was left of the tree trunks. Years later, all these thin, charred trees still stand like grey skeletons for miles and miles along the highway, right where we can see them – the Incorrupt Saints of the boreal forest world, or whatever. Something must be happening, some slow natural entropy that will eventually topple every one of them. It's probably hidden low, near the knee level of the burnt trees, where aspen saplings are reclaiming the land by inches every season.

It's hard not to wind up getting maudlin out here in The Old Burn, even though everyone in this country knows that wild forests are supposed to burn themselves up from time to time. It's a natural part of their life cycles, or something. Maybe making it into an analogy for the human condition is starting to get a bit trite. But you're pregnant right now, so you like the idea of things that can only be fruitful while they're being consumed. On good days, you don't mind that you live your life set on fire. The heat keeps you fine and fluid, white as molten steel. But on bad days, you are ash – grey and weightless, floating in the air over the dry old bones of the forest, drifting down onto the scorched spruce tendrils, moving only with the creaking of the dead trees.

"Are you getting sleepy?" I ask it in a near-whisper so the boys won't be disturbed.

"No danger of that," you answer. "You know I can't sleep in a car. Heck, I can hardly sleep in a bed these days."

I close my eyes and settle back into my seat. "Just let me know if you need me to do some driving."

"Nah, I'm good."

Just when it seems like any remnants of the civilization we've come from are long gone, you're waking me up to point out the big sign on the side of the road announcing the city limits. Beyond it, the forest opens up, and the highway falls into a valley made by an enormous river. It's called the Atha-basca. It's on its way out of the Rocky Mountains and into the Arctic Ocean, and it's wider than just about anything else like it on the continent. There're only two bridges spanning the Athabasca River inside the city. One goes north, to the petro-leum plants where I'll be spending nearly every day for the next five years. The other heads south, back to everyone and everything else we've ever known.

We find our new neighbourhood, up in the roads running in concentric circles on the wooded hills above the city's flood plains. It's a brand new trailer park where we've mortgaged a half million dollar strip of land with the mobile home bolted to it. Right now, my mother is still alive, down in the south of the province watching courtroom television and eating potato chips in her own trailer park. But her neighbourhood is noth-ing like this one. There's no vertical aluminum siding here – no harvest gold refrigerators, no peeling paper wood veneers, no orange shag carpet. Instead it's full of skylights and Jacuzzi tubs, walk-in closets, and guys who pay more in annual income taxes than my Dad has ever earned in a year.

We've arrived here a little too early to meet the realtor with the big white goatee – the man who has the keys to let us in-side our new home. But it's been a long drive, so we get out of the car anyway and walk around on the hard clay ground that was spread over this land – stiff and brown as refrigerated peanut butter – to fill in the unstable spaces where the muskeg used to be. The kids find a pile of boulders heaped behind the trailer and begin the serious work of climbing all over it. We sit on the wooden step built up to the back door out of new green arsenic-wood and wait for the realtor. I look down at my watch again. He is late now.

There's just the smallest trace of a smile around your mouth as you look up at me from the bottom step.

"Don't say it," I grin.

"I'm going to say it."

"Okay then."

"Mistah Kurtz, he dead."

In the narrow street, huge red and white buses – touring coaches kind of like the ones rock stars travel in – are roaring between the rows of diesel pickup trucks parked along the curbs. The open space in the centre of the asphalt is like the eye of a needle. And the buses thread themselves right through it, all over the trailer park, dropping off men still wearing hard hats and blue coveralls mucky with grease and striped with reflective safety tape.

One of the men from a rock star bus stamps up the stairs of the trailer next door – the one with the front door facing ours. He bawls out a greeting to us in a heavy Newfoundland accent. The sound of it brings out the borrowed Atlantic Canadian accent of your own, and in a few sentences you're talking way louder than you usually do, breathing in instead of out when you say "yeah," and referring to our trailer as "she."

I've just waved goodbye to him, and our new neighbour has one boot inside his trailer when we both stop and jerk our heads to look at you. You've let out this incredible, horror movie scream. Even our little boys have turned from where they sit on the boulder pile to see what's the matter with you.

"What is that?" you say, still almost in a yell. One of your hands has all your hair gathered into a ponytail while the other one is pointing at the ground, to the wooden planks laid down on the clay as a makeshift walkway.

The neighbour looks over and laughs – making it even harder for me to figure out what he's saying to us. I'll get used to the sound of accents like his soon, but for now I'm still ignorant enough for it to take two repetitions – each louder than the last – before I understand that he's identifying a big black bug sitting on the walkway. He calls it a tarsand beetle and claims it'll bite us.

I crouch as I creep up to the black creature waving its antennae on the walkway. It's a large beetle, all right. It's big enough that I might have believed someone if they'd told me it came here all the way from the Philippines. Its whole exoskeleton is matte black, as if it is truly made out of tar. What's most striking about it are its antennae. They're twice as long as the rest of its body, making the entire bug about five inches long in total from tip to tip. It's probably the biggest bug I've ever seen in Canada – but I still think you've overreacted.

I let you hear it in my voice. "For cryin' out loud–it's just a big beetle."

"Kill it!"

"Oh, for heck's sake. Someone's going to hear you screaming and call the police." I'm bringing my shoe down on top of the beetle. It's not even trying to get away. It just lies there, exposed, feeling up toward the sole of my shoe with its antennae.

The beetle's dead now so you let yourself get a little mad at me. "It–was–in–my–hair."

That is creepy. "But you're fine now," I say. "Aren't you?"

You just shudder.

There's a huge, mucus-white Cadillac SUV lumbering over the curb and into the yard. Its driver is our realtor. He's out of his vehicle and coming across the clay with a set of keys on one of his brokerage's fancy custom key fobs. He looks like he could be a Hollywood version of a plantation owner from the southern United States – but he's still just a northern boomtown realtor. He doesn't say anything when he sees the squashed tarsand beetle smeared by its ivory coloured guts against the wooden walkway – although he does take care not to step on it himself.

The bug stayed stuck to the wood for days afterward – long enough for you to start calling him "Gregor" and wondering out loud which of the oil sand projects he used to work at before he was changed.

We've been living in the city for a few months when one of the tarsand beetles finds his way ("Her way," you correct me, "the biggest ones are the females") inside our trailer. You're in the kitchen packing a lunch for me to take to "the plant" when I hear the bread knife hit the countertop as you start to scream. By the time I've spun around to see, you're standing by the counter in your undershirt. The T-shirt you were wearing is lying on the linoleum on the other side of the room.

The whole trailer shakes as I stomp back toward the kitchen. "What is it?"

"It's – in my shirt."

I let out a long breath. "Tarsand beetle." I stoop to gather up your shirt, heading to the back door where I'll shake out the bug and flick it back into the air.

The boys have come running and are standing at the edge of the kitchen, looking on with a fear a lot like your own. You never meant to do it, but you've made them afraid of the tarsand beetles too – though it's hard to take the boys seriously when they can't stop calling them "Tarzan beetles."

I'm standing in the doorway, calling back into the trailer over my shoulder. "It's okay, boys. Even the biggest beetle can't hurt you."

"Yes. Daddy's right. It can't hurt anybody. It just surprised Mummie." You force a little laugh. "Brigs – I am so stupid. I'm sorry."

I close the door and hand your shirt back to you. You hesitate but you take it, pinching the hem between two of your fingers like it's contaminated with some kind of biohazard now. I'm not surprised when you don't pull it back over your head. You're standing half-dressed in the kitchen, all flushed and ashamed. And I'm glad this happened at home, indoors, in private, because you would have done exactly the same thing if you'd seen a tarsand beetle perched on your shoulder, sorting through your hair, in the middle of a grocery store or at the park or in a restaurant or anywhere else.

I shake my head and pull you into me. "You've got to stop this."

"I know. I am so sorry." You're nodding against my chest. When I let you go, you throw your unsalvageable T-shirt into the laundry hamper.

As our first northern winter begins, all the bugs retreat into stasis somewhere in the forest. At the height of the cold half of the year, the daytime temperatures peak at no more than minus forty-five degrees Celsius. The snap lasts for two whole weeks without a break. It's so bad the steering fluid in the car freezes, and you keep Scottie home from kindergarten even though the schools are still open. The schools are always open. The scarcest resource in this town isn't money. It's childcare. There are some shift workers who will drop their kids off at the free-childcare utopia of the public school and head off to plants no matter what the weather. If those kids ever found the doors to the schools locked – well...

And then one day, while Scottie is away at kindergarten, you hear on the radio that his school is "in lockdown." At a construction site a few blocks from the schoolyard, a giant beetle appeared, looking exactly like a man. It scuttled into the cab of a bulldozer and bolted itself inside. They say it used to work for the contractor who owns the machine, so it's got keys, a stash of potato chips, a bottle of rye, and a sawed-off rifle it brought from home tucked under its puffy down coat that morning. Every few hours, the beetle fires off a shot, aiming into the frozen ground in front of the line of police cars that have gathered to pen him in. The shots keep the cops from losing interest in the standoff.

Desperate gunmen pirating heavy equipment – this is what it takes to get the boomtown school to finally lock its doors. You strap Aaron and baby Levi into the car, take the detour around the police barricades, and gather at the school with the rest of the moms who aren't at work themselves. None of you is afraid of the beetle's rifle, and together you stand in the snow banks outside the school, pulling on the doors, imagining your kids sitting under their desks inside, away from the windows.

Outside the school, it's like a meeting of surly mother bears.

"I bet they won't say a thing about this in the media," one of the other bears snuffles through her muzzle at you. "All the news up here cares about reporting is the price of shares at the plants."

Eventually, the principal cracks the front door and starts walking the kids out, bringing them to their mothers in small groups. The ones without parents in the crowd outside will just have to wait.

The beetle eventually burns off all the gas in the bulldozer. It shoots away all its rounds but one. And then it pleads with the police over its cell phone, asking them to go find the dowdy single mother who won't sleep with it anymore and bring her to the construction site so she can watch the beetle blast its brains out into the snow. The cops refuse to do it. Instead, they just arrest the beetle after the rye is all gone and the cold sets in.

Despite the months and months of cold, you never stop thinking about tarsand beetles. There's a handful of truisms we remember from our days as kids in school – something about fear being bred by ignorance. We do some research on tarsand beetles, hoping to cure this crazy phobic problem of yours.

"Don't call it 'hysteria,'" you warn me. "That's a sexist term."

Maybe you're right. But I never did try to call it hysteria.

"Okay. They're not actually called tarsand beetles," you explain as you turn off the computer. "And they never really eat tar. They're supposed to be called spruce sawyers."

"Well, that makes more sense." I wonder if you realize your hands are in your hair, fingering it, strand by strand, as you speak.

"And the guy next door was wrong. They won't bite people. They don't even try to eat anything that isn't part of a dead tree. They're actually a vital part of the forest ecosystem."

187

"Right."

"What they do is they lay their eggs underneath the bark of dead softwood trees once it starts to get cold in the fall. And then their larvae hatch in the spring and eat up a bunch of the wood. So they're helping to break down old trees and renew the soil. They're decomposers. They're helping."

I pull one of your hands away from your hair. "Of course they are."

You turn your hand so its fingers are holding onto mine. "And I bet you can guess what their favourite habitats are: areas where land has recently been cleared for new construction – which means everywhere, around here. Oh, and they also love land burned out by forest fires."

Forest fires – all those grey trees still un-fallen along the highway. They're standing out there waiting for your thick yellow hair to ride past them down the road, scattering the tar-sand beetles you've ferried from the city.

The city makes it through another winter. It's well into spring when I come home from work to find the bottom third of your hair is white. You were in the backyard painting the new fence with a sticky alkyd wood stain when a tarsand beetle flew right at your face – legs dangling under its belly, antennae laid back. It probably just came to see what was making that fantastic turpentine smell. When you heard the low, horrible buzz-flap of its big black wings, some mindless, electrical spark in your spinal cord ordered your arm to flinch. As always, the reaction was too violent and a tall, toxic plume of white paint came rising out of the can. It splashed against your back as you fled, destroying both your ratty old T-shirt and your braided rope of blonde hair.

At the salon where they cut off four inches of your hair, you tell your story to the stylist. She clucks her tongue as she tries to pull a comb through your hair. "No one likes dem, my love. Dey was the devil when we was kids."

"You had tarsand beetles back in Newfoundland?"

She shrugs into the mirror. "Well, we had June bugs. An' dey serves de same purpose."

When you're home again, I try to be gracious about the haircut but it does make me sad. I meet you at the front door, pushing your hood away from your face, sliding my fingers underneath what's left of your hair, up the length of your neck to where it starts to grow out of your nape. It's not just shorter. It's darker – made up of the new hair you've grown over the winter, since the light went away. All that's left are the strands that haven't been out in the sun long enough for their pigments to break down, lightening enough to lose that bamboo colour Janae used to call "dishwater blonde."

You won't look at me. "I had a lot of split ends that needed trimming anyway."

"What are we going to do with you?" I say. "These bugs aren't going anywhere. This is their natural environment. They've been here since before the dinosaurs. They're leftover from when this place was still the great big, hot jungle that made the oil sands in the first place."

But you don't apologize this time. Maybe you worked it all out in the hairdresser's chair. I don't know. Instead, you step away from me, opening the front door again, waving your arm toward the north.

Outside I hear the frogs creaking out some kind of love

song for each other in the bog behind the trailer park boundaries, beneath the black spruce trees. I'm used to the trees now. At first sight they make most people worry about what must have happened to those poor, deformed Christmas trees. They like to think it's pollution, or something. But the short, ragged limbs all covered in lacy swags of lichen, the prickly balls of tangled needles at the tops of the trunks – that's just what perfectly normal, healthy black spruces look like. It's rare to see one more than fifty feet tall since they usually burn to the ground every thirty years. But I've heard the aerial photographers at the plant say that up in the Athabasca River delta there are black spruces as tall as smoke stacks, growing in the safety of the little islands standing out in the water where the fires can never reach them. But those aren't the trees in our neighbourhood. There they are outside the window, growing in the spongy clouds of the sphagnum moss on the other side of the fire break the city has scraped into the clay in a wide, weedy swath behind our fence.

"Look out there. Do you see that?" you ask me. "That is the end of all human things. Those horrible little spruces go on and on and on out there, uninterrupted all the way up to the Arctic. And I'm in here with the baby and the little boys, looking out at it all day, every day. I'm just left here, wondering if the school's been locked down, or the bridge has gone out, or the forest is on fire again. So, Brigs, as long as we live here I have two options for managing my mental health –"

"Close the door. It still gets cold out there at night –"

"Listen. I can stop trying to fight back this bush fever, you know. I can give into it and let myself go crazy. I could go crazy. People here do it all the time. And then you'd have to get a flashlight and a hook and a big net to come pull me out of the muskeg and drag me back."

I know I shouldn't be laughing but I do it anyway.

"Or," you begin again, "or we can stick with the second option. I can keep on neatly consolidating all my anxiety and only resort to freaking out and screaming and running and destroying myself in the presence of that one big, nasty bug."

I take hold of the open door, gripping it high over your head. I'm pushing it closed when you stop me – standing in front of it, holding it open, rooting your feet into the floor and bracing the door open with your hip.

"The bugs aren't even nasty," I say. "You told me so yourself. Remember? Tarsand beetles are just spruce sawyers – part of the boreal ecosystem. And the worst thing they've ever done to you is bump into you long enough to make sure you're not a dead spruce tree who needs some help with your rotting – "

You gasp. "Rotting?" And then you pivot out of the open doorway and lunge into me, grabbing two fistfuls of my shirt. "Rotting?"

You're trying to shake me. It's got me laughing so hard I actually sway, knocking you sideways, stumbling past you, banging against the open door, slamming it shut.

# Twenty

We're here in the foyer of this dark brown downtown restaurant in the city, looking for Derek – your brother.

"He's going to order something boozy and drink it right in front of me just to see if I'll freak out at him," you warn us.

I reach down and squeeze your shoulder through your new pea coat. Because it was a gift I bought for you when you weren't around, the wool is dyed red. I know you never would have chosen it yourself. Derek will know it too.

I can hear you exhale as you open your cell phone and scroll through the list of incoming calls. "Where the heck is he?"

I nod and jerk my thumb at the door made of smoked glass in the wall beside us. "He's got to be in the bar."

You slump, sinking away from your red shoulders, shrinking even smaller. "Well, let's go in and find him then."

Behind the glass door, Derek is in the bar. He sees my large, pale face through the shadows as soon as I step inside, and he's waving at us from his seat in a corner. He's not drunk, but he is loud – though he's always been loud. We move toward him, surrounding his perch at a tiny, high table with a metal top cast to look like a manhole cover.

"Hey. Sit down. I wanna ask you something."

"Yeah? What?"

"I wanna know how your family history research is going." He's already asking even though you haven't finished climbing up onto the stool beside him.

It's a weird thing for him to ask. What does he care about all that obsessive family tree stuff anymore? It makes you mad. "Derek — I've got four kids under the age of nine to take care of all day long. They're incredibly time-consuming and I don't have a lot left for — "

"Hey, I'm not trying to make you feel lazy. It's just an innocent question."

"Sure."

"I'm asking because I ran into this guy, online — he's, like, Dad's second cousin once removed, or something — and he knows a ton about our family's roots."

"Great." You're nodding. "No, that's really great."

"Yeah. So anyways, this same guy made a trip all the way out to the Maritimes just so he could walk through the old graveyards taking pictures of all the headstones with familiar names on them."

We get it. It's just like it was when we went looking for Lost Caroline's grave, out there in the woods.

"And while he's out there, he finds the grave of our own great-grandfather. That's Dad's grandfather who — "

" — who died before Dad was even born so they never met," you interrupt. "I know that — we all know that."

"Right, but you don't know the rest of it yet." Derek is

leaning over the table like he's telling us a secret. "So the cemetery caretakers see Dad's cousin standing there, taking pictures of our great-grandfather's grave, and they come rushing right out to meet him – like he's a celebrity or something. And then they tell him the story." Derek gulps a mouthful of yeasty yellow grain juice from the glass sweating on the table in front of him. "See, right after the war, our great-grandfather's body was – exhumed. Did you know that?"

You sit back. "No. Why the heck would they do that?"

"Well, he was originally buried in some kind of charity plot for poor people, and when one of his sons finally made enough money to move him into the posh district of the graveyard, they went ahead and had it done. Caused a huge fight between all the brothers and sisters, but they did it anyway. And while the body was being moved," Derek glances behind us, "someone took a good look at it."

We're both frowning now. "At what?"

"At him – at the body."

"Somebody opened our great-grandfather's coffin – after burial?"

"Yup. It was ten years since he was first buried, and they opened it right up."

You cock your head to one side. "Why would anybody ever do that?"

Derek sits back and waves both his arms. "How the hell should I know?"

"I have no idea. But it's a fair enough question for me to ask, isn't it – "

"Then what happened?" I interrupt.

Derek takes another drink. "Right. So great-granddad's lying there inside the coffin, over ten years after they ran him through their shoddy, wartime embalming routine and buried him in the mud in the cheapest box they could find. And here's where the story gets – awesome. The caretakers told Dad's cousin that inside the coffin, the body looked like they'd just wheeled him off the hearse that morning."

You tilt your head to the other side.

Derek's tapping one fingertip against the tabletop in time with the words as he speaks. "Meaning, he didn't rot – all that time down there and he did not rot. They say his suit jacket had a little fuzzy white stuff growing on the lapel where a flower had been but otherwise he was perfect."

Now you're shaking your head. "Derek, that story isn't true. It's an urban legend those caretakers are passing on from second-, third- or fourth-hand accounts. And those stories must have already been exaggerated in the first place so – "

"I knew you were going to say that." He jabs his finger toward you. "But why? Short of driving across country and digging him up ourselves to take a second look, there's nothing we can do to prove it either way. Every word of what those caretakers said could have been absolutely true." He folds his arms across his front. "What do you make of it, Brigs?"

I clear my throat. "Must have been a cool, dry area they buried him in – at the start."

"Dry? In the poor people section of a Maritime graveyard? I don't think there's any such thing as a dry area in a place like that." Derek is talking to me but he nudges you with his elbow. And you're limp enough that you sway on top of your high stool when he touches you. "Oh, cheer up," he bawls at you. "Don't you get it? We are literal descendants of the undead. We're one-eighth vampire. These days that's got better social cachet than being one-quarter royalty."

You laugh so loudly a few of the other people in the bar turn to look. "Derek – you've been using this to meet women."

"And why not?" Derek slaps me on the back. "Vampires are smokin' hot, right Brigs? You know her well enough that you're not even surprised to hear what she really is, are you? You were just waiting for someone like a cemetery caretaker to stand up and expose us all, weren't you, Brigs?" He pokes you with his elbow again. "Look at him."

You do look at me. Your skin and hair and eyes – as always, there's hardly any pigment in any of them. The red of your coat reflects off your neck like it's a blank white screen. And I notice again how the skin in certain parts of your face – over your temples and around your eyes – is transparent enough for me to see the webs of blue veins that run beneath it.

But I just bow my head and laugh.

Derek waves his hand in your face. "Listen, forget about the vampire thing if you don't like it. Whatever. I just wanted to tell you all this because I know you've got that phobia about – rotting." He flicks a glance at me when he says it, like he's sorry. "And it's not that I don't get that. I do. I mean, I can't imagine what you guys must have – "

"It's okay," I shrug. "We're okay."

"But," he begins again, looking down at the top of your head, "don't – don't cremate yourself, okay? Burning is not the only way to get around rotting. You don't have to do it–"

You roll your head on your shoulders. "Derek – "

"–Because even after we die and get buried and everything, people like us – we won't necessarily have to end up like – like everybody else." This is where he silently tries to apologize to me again.

You're making that scoffing sound.

"Just – stop, okay," Derek blurts it out. "Quit being so greedy when it comes to death in the family. You act like you're the only one of us who knows anything about death – and it's not true."

You're not scoffing anymore. You're smiling into your hand. "Vampires," you say. "Here Derek, I've got something for you to look up on YouTube when you get home."

I already know what you're going to say. For some reason, it makes me sit up taller in my seat.

"Go home, get on YouTube, and type in a search for 'Incorrupt Saints.'" That's what you say as you slide off the edge of your barstool to stand on the floor.

But Derek's got one of those fancy computer cell phones and he's on the Internet already, right there in the bar. "Does 'incorrupt' have one R or two?"

"Come on, Brigs, let's get back to the boys," you're saying.

I lean close to him before I start to follow you out the door. "Hey, do you need any money?"

"Not this time. I'm good." He actually looks up from his screen and grins at me.

The video clip of the grainy still photos of the Incorrupt Saints is loading on the tiny computer screen suspended between his fingers. In a minute, its soundtrack will start to play.

It won't be the Eastern Orthodox chanting we heard in the version of the video that we watched at home. Instead it will be a maudlin Christian song, sung in a high tenor and in Tagalog, an urban Filipino language I never did learn to speak very well when I was living there, out in the jungles. The song will be loud, and Derek will curse and scramble to crank the volume into silence. But before it all starts, he has time to ask me one more thing. "Hey, keep her out of the furnace, would ya Brigs? Seriously..."

You don't turn around to look at us as you grab for the handle bolted to the smoked glass exit door. You're leaving but you're calling back to your brother as if the two of you are working on a crossword puzzle together.

"That's 'incorrupt' – with two Rs."

# Twenty-One

Maybe it's somewhere in the dark knots suspended in the blood. Maybe that was all it ever was – our never-born.

"I think I'm losing it," you say from behind the shaking curtains of your hair as I come through the door, textbooks falling to my feet. At the sight of you, I'm stomping right across the floor, leaving a path of mud and slush on the carpet. You've pulled your spine in, concave, and you're standing, leaning with both your hands on the edge of the kitchen sink.

All you say is, "It's bad."

I look for blood on the floor, on your legs and feet, but you've got something inside your clothes gathering it all – hiding it from me.

And I'm pivoting on the ball of one foot, spinning around before I reach you, moving back to the door. It's just to shut out the apartment building hallway outside. You're calling me back – no words, just sound – but I can hear that you think I'm leaving you too, as you stand, bowed over your womb cramping out its bright, secret blood.

"The door," I explain. "For your privacy–"

But everything in the apartment is already losing its colour along the edges of your vision. I've nudged the sickly ivory-coloured door firmly enough for it to move on its hinges in a slow arc, sweeping across your senses, wiping them out as it goes. You're slipping, your hands still clamped around the lip of the sink. The sounds in your ears are the final things to fade as the room washes white and disappears. And what you hear last of all is me, cursing as you hit the ground.

Our next pregnancy goes the distance.

And by the time it's nearly over, I hardly recognize you – even though you look almost exactly the same as you did before all of this. Actually, I'm working hard not to get freaked out by the way you never really "show." It's not like you're a big person or anything – not like those obese ladies who go to the hospital complaining about their gall bladders and then leave with perfectly healthy babies a few hours later. It's more like you keep it all held in tight with the force of your will alone. When I ask the doctor about it he tells me there's nothing wrong with you.

"What kind of ignorant man-question was that? Don't make me ban you from the doctor's office," you warn me later, in the car. These last few weeks you've been angry, almost constantly – except for during the times when you're sorry. But now you're leaning back in your seat, pulling your black T-shirt down tight over the thing and yelling, "Look at it. It's huge – like someone turned a pterodactyl egg upside down and rammed it up into my ribcage."

Packing the baby up that high inside your skeleton makes

you look like you've been holding in your breath ever since the night you led me by the hand into the dark and said, "Let's try it again. We've just got to get it over with. We'll be too poor to go anywhere or do anything 'til you're out of school anyway."

There is an argument in all of this that means something to me and – since you're mad all the time anyway – I'm going to rake it back to life. It's one of your favourite things to fight about, so I don't think you'll mind.

"They're going to ask me," I tell you. "The prenatal instructor said they're going to point the handles of those shiny, sterile scissors right at me and expect me to cut the cord."

You slam your palm down on the dashboard. "To cut *my* cord."

"*Our* cord. Half the DNA in it comes from me, doesn't it?"

"Half a cell, that's the most you can claim. The rest of it is made out of my meat." You're so gross sometimes.

"All dads cut the umbilical cords these days. They'll think there's something wrong with us if we don't do it too."

This is the part where you shout something about group-think and start to look like you want to punch me in the sternum. "How can you even ask me?" you're raving.

I try to laugh. "Look, someone's got to cut it eventually. You can't just leave him hanging there."

"That's right, Brigs. The doctor cuts it. When he does it, we can all tell ourselves it's clinical. If you do it, there's no way to argue it's not political. I can't think of a better example of patriarchal violence than you cutting through my flesh to tear my baby away."

"But letting me do it gives me a real role in this. Even if it's all just ceremonial, it gives me something to do – "

"*Do*? You can't *do* anything. Not here."

This is the part where I bend over the steering wheel until my head touches the horn. If I'm reckless I might mutter something about feminist baggage. And I'll wonder if you'll have any sympathy for me if I try to be tender and entreat you to let me join in with this amazing creation thing you've got going on. But whenever I choose that road you just laugh – cold and hard – and remind me of all the times you couldn't get new jars of spaghetti sauce open.

"Come on, Brigs. We each have to come to terms with the physical limitations of our sex someday."

Here at the hospital, at the end, they've got you doped up on something. You're brushing cobwebs off your face that just aren't there. I ask you if it still hurts and you grab me by the shirt, pull me into you, and then throw me back again. I'm not sure if you can still talk.

I asked you once about that new thing they do where they thread a tube into the spine and shut everything down from the middle of your back to the tips of your plain pink toenails. It sounds pretty good to me.

"It would," is what you said at the time. "If men birthed their babies themselves, that's the kind of technology that would have been invented before the frickin' wheel."

I thought you meant you wanted to have it done yourself.

But then you just got even madder. "How can you suggest that I call a man in a white coat to alienate me from my body precisely at the point in time when it's at its most powerful?"

That was your last word on it. Maybe I should have asked you if it would still be patriarchal violence if the doctor who did it was a woman. But I didn't. It felt like a landmine at the time. And I think it's too late to mention it to any of the hospital people now – even though it's getting harder and harder to keep all this fear off my face when you look at me.

And now in the hospital, after all these weeks, you're not angry anymore – and it's really scaring me. You're not even angry at the nurse, standing on the opposite side of the bed-chair thing from me yelling, "Push harder, push harder," right into your face for two hours straight – like you've got something more important to do later in the day and you're trying to save your strength for it.

"Lady," I finally have to say. "Cool it, okay?"

We've been here almost a whole day and I think I'm getting good at reading the output from the electronic fetal monitor. You'll tell me later you've got a post-traumatic stress reaction to the sound pounding out of the machine.

*Kee-ow-wow-wow-wow, Kee-ow-wow-wow-wow*

I ask the doctor if the strength of your contractions will ever get stronger again after they start to wane, like I can see yours are doing. He says, no.

You want to tell me you're dying. Somehow, I know that's what you'd say to me if you could. And if you told me so yourself, out loud, I would believe you. I can see it's true in your face, where a thousand tiny, rusty bruises have bloomed – as if the pores in your skin are about to start bleeding, right around your eyes.

But instead of letting you die, they call this old specialist doctor. He comes into the hospital room with a set of long, curved tongs like something from the Inquisition. He cuts and thrusts and pulls and out comes the whole thing. That's when I know for sure you can't talk – not with language anyway. Your voice is a landslide.

There must be seven people in the room by the end, all twitching for disaster, tearing open packages, rubbing, sucking, and making the same notes over and over again.

"No. No again. No, she's still not allergic to anything."

When they give me the lavender baby I walk it over to where they're sewing your birth canal back together for me with a long, fish-hook needle each of us is taking pains not to look at. The baby is a boy, like you wanted. He's wide awake.

Your voice is wordy again but low and wrapped in cotton. "I couldn't see," you say to me. "I couldn't see anything. Did you get to cut it?"

At least I have this to give you. "No."

And that – for the first time in this, the longest of all the days of creation – is when you cry.

Maybe it would have been easier at first if the baby had been born as a dinosaur out of your pterodactyl egg – a gigantic, toothy reptile that could walk and forage and lapse into sleepy, cold-blooded stasis without much help from you. But he's far too big for that. Instead, he's come to you like an eclipse of the sun – more vast than anything, crushing you into the gravity of the endless revolutions of his need.

Of course, you understand what it all means before I do. He's still just barely born when I notice you won't say his name above a whisper in the hospital in case the nurses or the janitors or – anybody – hears you.

"It doesn't seem right for us to be able to just start calling him whatever we want," you say. "Our name for him – it's so arbitrary. I mean, we just made it up."

I remind you of what you told me once about our names being social constructs. "It's how we show he belongs to us, remember? Out on the bridge that night?" I pause to assemble your old arguments. "Our names only exist outside ourselves. We don't even bother to use our names in our dreams, when we're asleep. Right?"

But you still look a little scared as you shrug one shoulder. Me and the baby – we've each changed your name. When we got married, I got you to abandon the surname you'd been known by for your first twenty-one years. And without a word, the baby now demands that you call yourself something like "Mom." He's taken everything. Even a real dinosaur would have spared more.

At home, after dark, you are a ghost – a small, pale ghost rising from my bed in the night; walking over the carpet with bare, white feet; twisting the door knobs in the dark; grappling with the mass of snuffling, sticky humanity I call "Scottie" in the daylight – as if I know him. You stand away from me, in the quiet of the living room, swaying with the baby in the dark until the shabby apartment carpet starts to close over your toes and heels. The hallucination startles you awake on your feet, over and over again.

In the morning, when I ask how you've both slept, you tell me – hour by hour – how it all passed. And I listen, trying to stop my features from forming into the blank, sceptical face of any grown man listening to a ghost story.

"This nursing thing has got to be a sham," you tell me.

"Feel my breast. No – not like that. Like this. Do you feel that? It's not full of milk. It's packed with pebbles."

"No, no." I make a bright protest. "Look at how well he's growing. You can't build a boy like that out of pebbles."

You bend to kiss the baby's silky head where he lies on the bed between us, waving his hands and fanning his fingers as if he's trying to maintain some kind of complicated magic spell over us. I don't know how you can keep from hating him, and I'm always relieved to see you kiss him or make some other kind of small display of your unlikely affection for him. Sometimes, I worry that it's all just Stockholm Syndrome. But then I decide that, for now, Stockholm Syndrome will do well enough.

Outside the apartment, there are term papers for me to write about fluid dynamics and kinematic determinacy. There are study groups full of paper cups and expensive calculators. There are labs and lecture halls – hard math classes and hard math classes called by other names. So I leave you, all day long. And for all but a few harried hours in the evening, my life looks remarkably similar to the one I lived before the eclipse of the sun – the end of your world.

You mourn your lost self. She leaks out in millilitres from your eyes every day at three o'clock in the afternoon.

"She's gone for good and as good as dead," you tell me. "She's gone and I never realized before how much I loved her."

Remember how badly it all scared me? Remember how I hid all the Radiohead CDs and looked up the number for the postpartum help hotline in the telephone book?

"Don't be stupid," you say as you push the phone book back against my chest. "I'd be more worried about my state of mind if something like this failed to upset me." And you show me a reference to something with the diminutive, flippant label of "baby blues" in the index of our dog-eared pregnancy and childbirth manual.

In all the years that follow, we never speak about the afternoon when you nurse the baby to sleep on our bed, tuck yourself back into your clothes, kiss my face, and tell me you're going out to buy bread and eggs. You drive to the grocery store, walk the aisles, pay our money – but you don't come home. You steer the car all the way through the city until you find an unfamiliar stretch of freeway charging northward. It leads you past the greasy architecture of the eastside refineries, the candy striped smoke stacks, the flaming orange gas flares.

Finally, the road splits. You choose the obscure exit and end up crossing a railway track, bouncing onto the gravel road leading between barbed wire gates and into an enormous garbage dump. This is the landfill we and our one million closest neighbours have been packing with our refuse. Our little car bangs in and out of the deep, sun-hardened mud ruts in the roadway. Behind the gates, you drive over the massive weigh scale – "dead slow," the sign says. You are weighed and measured and, you have no doubt, found wanting.

And in the household refuse rubble field, at the edge of the mound of bedsprings, Chinese particle board, and black plastic, you cut the engine and step out of the car.

The air reeks like the inside of a warm, dirty refrigerator, but you sit on the edge of the hood, right out in the open anyway. The dump is patrolled by ravens too big and bearded to be mistaken for common crows. They're the kind of birds we usually only see in the mountains or way up north. You watch them tossing and tearing plastic bags with the long knives of their black beaks. You're wondering where their chicks are right now. None of the birds on the trash mounds look anything but old and hoary. Maybe there are no such thing as raven chicks, and the birds just spring to life without any infancy – incarnated fully grown from tattered black garbage bags caught in tree branches and held there, rustling through enough winters to be blown into enormous, shaggy birds.

The weary beeping of bulldozers' back-up signals sound from behind the incomprehensible trash-mountain heaped in front of our car. Some of the ravens answer back a mimicking cry. Their voices make you smile – even though you know they're carrion birds and they'd merrily strip your body down to its bare bones if you sat too still for too long.

You stay there, perched on the hood of our car parked on the sandy ground in front of the trash-mountain, until your breasts ache and harden beneath your tightly folded arms. It tingles and stings, as if you can feel each of the rough, tiny crystals that move though the glands and ducts beneath your skin. Maybe you could stay there, behind the barbed gates, until the milk runs down through the fabric of your shirt and onto your arms, along the metal curves of the car, dripping to where it would fall to darken the dirt below you. You wouldn't need to cut yourself to spill it. The milk drains out of your body all the same, through openings in your skin that you can't even see – smaller than pores. You always said your milk was so pretty – like liquefied ivory when it stood on our newborns' fuzzy cheeks. It's probably the same colour as the bones from which it was drawn – your bones, delicate and beautiful and unsee-able except for the bits of them suspended in your milk.

You'll never tell me how you thought about doing it – about sitting dead still on the hood of the car. Maybe, in time, the ravens would have forgotten what you really were – and you would have stopped worrying about it. And the birds would have come hopping toward you, moving sideways, peering at you around their broad blind spots with each of their shiny, black eyes in turn. But even if they mistook you for dead, they wouldn't have eaten you – not your flesh. They would have inched close enough to peck at the ground where your milk would have been spilt in the dirt, still warm – great, shaggy black birds swallowing, brown grit and ivory milk, all at once.

You don't stay in the city dump long enough to find out any of this. You come back to us – to the baby and me and the future full of his brothers. I hope I know why – but I can never be sure.

It's been hours since you left. Still, I don't ask any dangerous questions about where you've been. "Did you enjoy your break?" is what I decide to say in the cheerful voice I've been practicing.

Even this makes you wince. Your arms are outstretched anyway. "Give him here. He needs to eat."

"He's not crying – "

You're pulling at your clothes anyway. "Well, *I* need him to eat. I guess this relationship isn't quite perfectly parasitic."

You take the baby and sit down on the couch, bending yourself into your typical, awkward nursing posture that made all the lactation consultants frown. There's a pillow across your lap, your spine is stooped so your head sits too far forward, one of your elbows is thrust out at me like a lesser-than sign, and you're offering yourself to our child.

And even through every offering you make, we both know the baby himself is not really an idol. He's just an altar – a place to lay sacrifices. The sacrifice you make here is so profound I've never dared to mention my own – real but lost and invisible in the face of the cataclysm of your new motherhood. But the look of sameness in the routine of my life is not real. I have laid something precious on the altar of the baby too. My own sacrifice – it was you.

# Twenty-Two

He's stooped over the plain white sink, washing his hands from the last throat swab of the day when his receptionist leans into the exam room. "I am so sorry," she begins, "but we've got a bit of a problem out front."

He raises his head but doesn't look at her – he never looks directly at them. "Hm?"

"There's this – lady – sitting right up on top of the appointment desk. I'm pretty sure she's not a patient but she's come barging into the clinic right at closing, no appointment or anything, and tells me you have to see her, right now."

"Not a patient." He repeats it as if he already understands.

He's still wiping his hands on a paper towel as the receptionist tells him the name of Brigs's wife. Someone from their old high school class has already been into this doctor's clinic that morning for a prenatal appointment. That was where the doctor had been sitting – bent over, rubber-gloved, stunned, and penned between the stirrups of an exam table – when he first heard what happened to Brigs, a man he only met once, a man married to someone he used to love. Since then, the doctor has had this feeling, all day long, like he should be expecting a visit.

The receptionist sees the doctor's throat ripple beneath his nodding head.

"I can always send her away," she offers. "I told her I wasn't sure if you'd left for the day or not. I can go tell her it's too late –"

"No." He shakes his head. "It's okay. Send her into my office."

He crosses the hall, flicks on the brass lamp his wife bought him for Father's Day, and sits down behind stacks of drug manuals, bending himself into a wheeled leather chair a lot like the one in Brigs's office. He takes in a deep breath, closes his eyes, and tips his head back as he exhales, like a meditation.

That's how Brigs's wife finds the doctor – her once and former prom date – when she comes to stand in the open doorway of his office, her feet apart, her hands on her hips. "What are we doing in here, Dan?" she's demanding.

He jolts. "Carrie – hi. This is my office, where I do counselling."

"Well, get up," Carrie says, lunging forward and pushing the arm of his chair hard enough to spin it a half-turn away from her. "We need to be in an exam room for this."

As he rises, she's already twisting the knob of a numbered door in the wall beside his office. "This one will do, right?"

He's behind her. "Sure."

"Good." The door swings open with a bang.

"Yeah, I heard what happened – with your husband's accident. I can't begin to say how sorry I am."

"Thanks." She's standing in the centre of the tiny room – between the padded, papered table and another one of those tiny, white sinks – scanning the countertops as if she's looking for something.

"Hey," he says, closing the door. "I feel like you want me to do something for you besides be sorry. But I'd rather not try to guess what it is. You can just tell me."

"Can I?" She pulls open a drawer in the small cabinet bolted to the floor. It's one of the old ones from when the clinic was new. It's made of tin and painted with white enamel. Its top drawer is full of individually wrapped alcohol swabs and long, wooden Q-tips in sterile packages.

He doesn't interfere as she opens a second drawer. "Look, Carrie, I know you must be devastated. And I want to help you. But I can't do anything if you just keep ransacking my clinic without actually talking to me."

She grasps the handle of the last unopened drawer in the cabinet. It doesn't move. "Locked," she says. "This must be the right one then. Where's the key, Dan?"

"You have to tell me what you're looking for."

She sighs and rolls her head from one shoulder to the other. "Okay, I need a good scalpel – not one of those hack jobs like they gave us to use in zoology labs back in school. I need a good one like you'd use to operate on a real person."

He answers with a tense, unvoiced laugh.

"And I might need some advice too," she continues. "I mean, I imagine it's probably a lot like de-boning a chicken. But I've never exactly done this sort of thing before – on a person."

"What? You mean – surgery?" he says.

"Yes."

That disorienting feeling she used to give him in high school is coming back to him now. Here is it again – the same almost giddy exhaustion and confusion she always trailed behind herself when it came to him. And he's defending himself against it the same way he always did in the past: by patronizing her.

He shakes his head like he's trying to wake up. "Let me get this straight: you drove all the way down here – at a time like this – so you could get me to give you a scalpel and – " He glances down, looking right at her face. "What exactly is it you're going to do?"

They look into one another's faces for an instant, the way they never used to do when they loved each other. And if she ever loved anyone before Brigs, out of all the other boys, this was who it was – this is Brigs's forerunner. Maybe that's the real reason why she's come here, not even twenty-four hours after Brigs died. She's trying to rediscover the beginning of the way that leads back to her husband.

It happens so fast the doctor doesn't even sense that she's reached her hand out, snatching at his hand until she's already holding it in both of her own. His hand is smaller than Brigs's, over-washed, and cold. In this small town with its one doctor's office, there isn't anyone for miles who doesn't know the doctor's hand by now. For a second, he thinks she might just want what all the other widows want when they come to see him, and he closes his fingers around hers, loosely, in that clinical, comforting hold of his.

But she's tracing a line down the back of his hand, firm and straight – marking the bone that runs from his wrist to his first knuckle. "I want one these," she says. "Not yours," she hurries when she feels him jerking away. "I want one of these bones from Brigs's hand. Don't worry, I asked him ages ago if I could have one. He said I could take it. I'm pretty sure he said so."

When she knows Dan understands, she drops his hand. Now that it's free, he holds his hand up under the fluorescent lights and looks for the invisible trace of the line she's drawn on his skin. "You want me to give you a scalpel and a – tutorial – so you can cut a bone out of your deceased husband's hand."

"Yes. Well, ideally you'd come with me and cut it out of him yourself –"

He steps back, until his spine is pressed against the closed door.

"But I know that's too much to ask so – so, here I am."

He hooks the bottom of a wheeled stool with his foot. "Sit down," he tells her.

"I don't have a lot of time – "

"Sit down, Carrie," he repeats, sitting on the stool himself. She obeys and he wheels his seat over to the chair she's chosen. He leans his elbow on her chair's metal arm. "Look, everyone grieves in his or her own way. I counsel a lot of people and I've learned to respect that. I've seen some bereaved people who shut right down and can't do anything. And I've seen other people who get – manic."

"You think I've gone crazy."

His chin droops to his chest. "I think you're beside yourself – and understandably so. But you can't go carving up your husband for comfort. Cutting doesn't bind, it breaks. I honestly think this kind of operation couldn't possibly do anything but upset you even more. And – and it's not appropriate."

"Appropriate – what the hell does that mean?"

"It means that people will come to the viewing and wind up having to deal with seeing his hand is all – tampered with. Someone could quite possibly call the police."

She doesn't hesitate. "Tampered with? It's not like the organ procurement people haven't already picked though him. He hasn't exactly got pristine remains anymore. Besides, if I have him cremated, no one will ever be able to tell what has or hasn't been tampered with."

The doctor glances over his shoulder and lowers his voice. "But the body is sacred, Carrie. You know that. We don't keep physical souvenirs of human bodies rattling around with the living."

She sits up straight in her chair. "They do in the Philippines. Brigs had whole pages of pictures of Philippine cemeteries in his photo album. Their graveyards are full of piles of dry bones sorted into heaps – skulls over here, femurs over there. And they're just stacked up, like firewood or cannon balls, resting on top of the crypts and between the crosses."

"But isn't that just a vestige of poverty? I mean, people might be used to it and they're making the best of it but that doesn't mean it's an ideal situation."

She rolls her eyes. "Ethnocentric much?"

He ignores it. "And don't forget that you still have something literal left over from Brigs himself. You have all those fine heirs you produced for him."

He's trying to be sweet – trying to make her laugh – but she throws herself backward into her chair, like she's disgusted. "Don't give me that living-on-through-his-children nonsense. The boys are not him. They're themselves. And their destiny has always been to leave me."

The doctor sits back too, and a silent moment passes while they both hate each other. "Why don't you let me give you something to help you sleep instead?" is what he finally offers.

"I can write you a prescription and you can take what you need until you're calm and rested and thinking more clearly." He's already scrawling something on a prescription pad. He's using the same serial killer handwriting he had back in university.

"Sleeping pills do not work on me." She's wrenching his pen away from him, throwing it over his shoulder, against the closed door. There's a tiny knock just as the pen hits the wood, as if someone has been listening from the outside, waiting to break in once they were sure Carrie had snapped. The door opens and the receptionist sticks her head inside the room.

"Everything okay?" she sings.

"Yeah, it's fine," the doctor answers. "You can go now. We'll see you tomorrow."

But the receptionist just stands there.

"Really. It's okay. Please go."

She leaves but the door stays ajar.

Carrie jumps to her feet and slams the door. She's spinning around, pulling at the locked drawer again, asking, "So, would it be better for me to cut in first at the wrist or at the knuckle – or in between?"

The doctor sighs and shakes his head.

She kicks at the cabinet hard enough to leave a dent in its side. "I don't need you for this, you know. I'm still a very re-sourceful girl and I could get this done with nothing but a ra-zor blade from my toolbox, flashbacks from zoology class, and what would probably amount to some pretty gruesome trial and error."

The doctor has spun his stool around to look at her. "Just snip off a lock of his hair – "

"Not good enough."

"Or a sliver of his fingernail – "

"Gross."

"Carrie – "

"No, keep going, Dan. You're getting closer. The next thing is to suggest I pull out one of his teeth."

The doctor sighs again and runs both of his hands through his own hair. He pulls back, shocked, when he feels her hand in his hair too. Carrie is standing right next to him and she's teased out one short, white lock from the rest of the dark brown strands. "Look at it," she says in a moan. "Your hair – it really is getting grey."

He looks up as she drops her hand away. "Don't do it," he says. "I'm asking you – please. Don't cut him. You can't lawfully do it. It says so right in the Criminal Code."

"But the bone – all that time – it was him, it was mine, wasn't it? And even now, isn't it still mine?" And that's when she starts to cry. He's been waiting for it – almost wishing for it – but it hits him right in the guts anyway.

She sits down on the floor of the exam room, her knees bent up to her eye level, sobbing, with both her palms pressed against her eyelids.

And the doctor is nodding and patting her knee in a familiar, doctor-ly pantomime of compassion. But then she's sliding away, rising to kneel on the dingy white tiles at his feet. He sits back, gaping down at the head of blonde hair slumped against the side of his leg. He's not sure if it's real but he thinks he might be able to smell something – sweet like the rosewater she used to dab in her hair when she was his.

"Please," she begs against his shin.

"Carrie – come on, now. Get up. Carrie – Caroline – don't."

"Please, Dan – please. Help me. I can't risk ending up with nothing."

She's sobbing too hard to hear his last sigh – the one where he empties his lungs right down to their tidal volume. He glances up at the exam room door to make sure it's firmly latched before he takes a small key from the ring in his pocket, leans toward the cabinet, and unlocks the one drawer she couldn't open. And then he's on his knees too, down on the floor in front of her, pushing her upright, gripping her wrist, pulling her hand away from her face. He's holding something wrapped in a small, stiff rectangle of heavy, sterile foil. He's pressing it into her palm, finally ready to make the offering.

"Lead with the curved edge, not with the tip," he says. "Don't stab. Slice."

## Twenty-Three

Remember that book we used to read to the kids – the one where it's promised that, in the end, no one is told any story but their own? After all I've said here, I guess it must not be true. Or maybe it's just that we lived our lives together well enough to make the story of me into the story of you. And then again, maybe there is only one great, inextricable story – the story of everyone the whole world over. As it turns out, it's all the same.

But even though everything's clear to me now – all the smirks and sighs, every word of every uncle and cousin, the insides of your teeth and bones – I can hardly see you as you are at this moment. I need to stop trying. I know that. You will arrive. And the wait won't be too long – not like it will seem to you.

Still, I stoop and strain to watch you through the mounting dimness of these fine new eyes. You are closed inside a house, sitting at a kitchen table, hemmed in by stacks and stacks of widow's paperwork. The federal government wants my social insurance card back – sealed in an envelope and mailed across the country to be officially obliterated. The address for the office is in New Brunswick, about an hour's drive from Butcher Hill.

I want to reach through everything in between and lift the hair falling down your back. I want to see if there's any trace of it – the clasp of a chain, the tied ends of a leather strap – anything to show if you got the token, the bone, you once asked me to give to you out of the top of my hand. There's nothing in the hand I have now to tell me.

You must know – in the end, I would have given it, freely, if I'd been able.

And there are other questions. I could still see long enough to know that the accident didn't leave my body mangled. It was a hard impact from one side – a steel bumper jammed into the door of my car as the truck driver of the apocalypse failed to yield to me at a stop sign, or something. It rocked me with a sideways whiplash, sending the sharp edge of my own vertebrae cutting through the nerves in my neck that keep me breathing and beating. My heart and lungs waited and waited between my ribs, beneath the breach – perfect and whole and suddenly and completely forgetful of everything they used to do and why they ever did it.

It's not like it was with my dead mother. The ambulance was there in minutes, even though the truck driver was standing shaking on the pavement and there was nothing they could do for me. I died instantly and beautifully. Everyone tells you so, over and over again. You could have buried me face up on a satin pillow, mouth pressed into a gentle smile at the head of a casket, a little swollen in the neck but completely unburnt. My body could have been made into a museum exhibit, enshrined in a cathedral – or simply filed underground if you'd changed your mind and decided you wanted it that way. I just don't know. Maybe after all the fussing, it was never very important how you got rid of what was left of me.

Whatever happened to the art of casting full facial death masks? I can remember the pictures I've seen of Napoleon's death mask – and Lincoln's and Joseph Smith's and Isaac Newton's. As far as I know, the closest thing there is to a death mask of me are those dental impressions they needed in order to make the mouthguard that was supposed to keep me from grinding my teeth away in my sleep. Maybe you remembered those plaster teeth and gums, wrapped in bubbled plastic on the top shelf of the bedroom closet. Maybe they satisfied your need for my body, and you didn't try to take a bone from my hand after all.

I look at the hand I have now and I still can't tell.

But I can see into your lowest point of this valley. I am watching, somehow, the night after the funeral as you stand in the backyard, out of the range of the square eye of yellow light coming through the kitchen window onto the lawn. And my brother's wife stands with her hand on your waist while he clamps you in arms so much like my own they could almost wrap around you twice. And he bows his head over you and smothers your face into the front of himself as if your grief is a fire for him to crush into extinction. And your mouth is full of his black, hooded sweatshirt as you wail into him – unheard by our sons, or my last parent, or anyone else who could not abide the day.

"Carrie," he rumbles, "I'm sorry. I'm not Brigs."

"No," you answer. "I am."

## Acknowledgements

It seems like most people who finish a book and sell the manuscript have either already raised a family or haven't started to raise one yet. The rest of us have very patient, understanding, and indulgent spouses and children. I must acknowledge these traits in Anders and in our sons, Jonah, Samuel, Nathan, Micah, and little James who was just three years old when I finished the first draft of this novel. Thanks, boys.

And thanks to my publisher, Linda Leith, for including me in her brave new venture. I must also acknowledge the memories of my nearest kindred dead: Bob McCarthy, Ralph and Thelma MacKenzie, and especially Bryan Quist. Thank you for cradling me in your lives and in your deaths.